THE GIRL REVEALED

THE GIRL REVEALED

THE LAST VAMPIRE™ BOOK 6

JUDITH BERENS   MARTHA CARR   MICHAEL ANDERLE

Copyright © 2019 Judith Berens, Martha Carr and Michael Anderle
Cover by Fantasy Book Design
Cover copyright © LMBPN Publishing
A Michael Anderle Production

LMBPN Publishing
PMB 196, 2540 South Maryland Pkwy
Las Vegas, NV 89109

First US edition, September 2019
eBook ISBN: 978-1-64202-458-6
Print ISBN: 978-1-64202-459-3

THE GIRL REVEALED TEAM

Thanks to the JIT Team

Misty Roa
Angel LaVey
Larry Omans
Paul Westman

If we've missed anyone, please let us know!

Editor
SkyHunter Editing Team

From Martha

To everyone who still believes in magic
and all the possibilities that holds.
To all the readers who make this
entire ride so much fun.
And to my son, Louie and so many wonderful friends who
remind me all the time of what
really matters and how wonderful
life can be in any given moment.

From Michael

To Family, Friends and
Those Who Love
To Read.
May We All Enjoy Grace
To Live The Life We Are
Called.

CHAPTER ONE

The windows of Coach Lueck's classroom rattled. Heavy rain pelted the glass and filled the room with a tapping sound that almost drowned out the voices inside.

"Boy, that thunder won't let up, will it?" Krista shook her head as she looked out at the dark gray clouds that loomed overhead.

Her teammate, Wendy, smiled as she gathered her shoulder-length hair into a tight ponytail. Her crystal-blue eyes twinkled, even on the grayest of days. "It's been pouring all day. Why would it stop now?"

She pursed her lips together. "I was kinda hoping we wouldn't have to run in this today."

Where she stood behind them with her arms folded, Vickie arched her eyebrows quizzically. "Will Coach really make us run in this?" It didn't bother her too much to run in the rain but she assumed a normal human body would have a hard time with it.

Wendy laughed. "Coach thinks runners are like the

British mail carriers. Whether snow, or sleet, or rain, or shine… It doesn't matter what the weather is like outside."

"It's a badge of honor for runners." Krista turned away from the window. "Football players have practice inside on days like these. So do soccer players, tennis players, whoever…but the runners still head out there and brave the weather."

The three of them wandered to some open desks and sat to wait for the standard pre-practice pep talk from Coach Lueck before they all departed for their daily runs. The lights flickered slightly after another crash of thunder boomed.

Micah, one of the boy runners, laughed loudly. "Only in Wisconsin can you get a foot of snow followed by a monsoon in the same month." A few other students laughed.

"All right, all right." Coach Lueck bounded into the room with his usual wild enthusiasm. "It looks like a great day for a run, everyone." A few of the team groaned. "Now, now. None of that. Other teams can take a break or move inside. Not us. There's no reason why we can't go out there and get a good few miles in. However, safety is an issue. I've watched the skies all day today and it hasn't been too violent out there. There's fairly heavy rain, but that's about it. If you see excessive lightning, feel free to turn and come back. Otherwise, gut it out and have some fun. This is the joy of running right here."

Once they were dismissed, the girls stood in front of the tall glass doors leading outside and stared at the sky. Buckets of rain still emptied relentlessly.

"It looks like it's almost midnight out there," one girl

commented.

"We'll be soaked the second we step outside," another muttered.

But they had their assignment and they were expected to get out and pound the pavement. Taking a collective deep breath, they all ventured out into the rain.

Wendy led the group that day and shouted instructions. "We'll head to the creek!" she yelled in an effort to not to get drowned out—both literally and figuratively—by the rain. "We need to stay off the road when it's this dark."

The small stream ran parallel to the Honey Creek Parkway. It was designed to help keep roads from flooding, so once they moved past the dirt path and the trees, they could actually run on the concrete banks of the waterway. On sunny days, the team could run three or four runners wide in a tight pack.

But when they reached what was left of the concrete banks after they'd all but sloshed through the muddy path, Krista observed loudly what they all saw. "Holy cow. We'll be lucky to run two runners abreast."

Sure enough, the rushing, crashing waters of the creek had risen substantially from all the rainfall of the day-long downpour.

"Okay, everyone. One at a time." Wendy led the way and the girls fell into a rhythm, single-file, behind her.

As predicted, their feet squished through wet socks. Shirts and shorts clung tightly to their bodies, and strands of hair plastered to their foreheads as they pushed on through the sheets of rain that showed no signs of abating.

Another crash of thunder rumbled ominously. Vickie slid deliberately into the middle of the pack as violent weather had a tendency to spark her fight-or-flight response. Every time they were surprised by the roll of thunder, her fangs poked her tongue and a rush of energy surged through her.

By running in the middle of the pack, she could ensure that she wouldn't accidentally sprint past anyone thanks to her super-speed.

But several minutes in, her stomach twisted. *Uh oh. Is this coming from the rain or something else?* She took a few deep breaths and scanned the area. *There doesn't seem to be anything around here. Everyone is paying attention to what they're doing. We're fine.*

Normally, a review of her situation and a few deep breaths could get the feeling to subside after a minute or two. But as they continued, the sensation nagged at her and her stomach twisted tighter. *This isn't from the thunder. Something is happening.*

The vampire looked at the waters that rushed past them. They jogged in the upstream direction and the waters flowed the opposite way. *It's the water. Something's in the water. I need to get away quickly.*

She stepped off to the side and looked at Krista, who was a few runners behind her as she let them pass. "I'll be right back. I'll catch up." Her friend nodded with a confused look but didn't spare the time to really think about it.

Vickie jogged in the other direction—downstream—and glanced back to make sure the team was out of sight. She was briefly thankful for the heavy rains which concealed her sooner than a sunny day would.

Allowing the rush of energy to power her, she sprinted

away in super-speed and studied the water carefully. Seconds later, she came across a set of fingertips that peeked out from the water before they submerged again. If it hadn't been for her vampire-heightened senses, she would've missed them.

Without another thought, she barreled into the current and ran with the tide pushing her forward. To her surprise, the level eventually grew deep enough that she was in over her head, so she took a deep breath and ducked under to swim as fast as she could until she finally encountered a body that drifted—apparently lifelessly—along.

It was not a small body at all. She expected it to be a child, but it was about her size, if not a touch larger. Fortunately, the size was no challenge to her strength and she wound her arms around the person and pulled them to the side while she fought the current.

Once she had a solid footing on the concrete, she hoisted the body out of the water completely and dragged it out of the creek and onto the muddy banks beyond the cement.

She lowered the body and studied the teenage boy. Vickie didn't recognize him, but she checked his pulse. *He still has a heartbeat, so he's okay.*

About to check his breathing, she was surprised when he snapped awake. His eyes opened and he took a few deep breaths. He appeared confused that he was out of the water as he heaved for oxygen and the rain washed the dirty creek water off his face.

"Are you okay?" she shouted.

"I'm fine. Thank you." The boy still had a spooked expression.

"I thought you were drowning."

"Me too. I can't swim. I was down here looking at the creek and I slipped and fell in. I can't swim, so I couldn't fight my way out." He sat and stared at the rushing water. "I honestly thought I would die."

"You're okay now. Can you get out of here without falling in again?" Vickie didn't mean to sound like she was treating him like a child. He was clearly in high school, but she also didn't want her efforts to go to waste. Fortunately, he didn't seem to notice.

He smiled. "Don't worry. I won't go back in. I promise. I'll go straight up to the street and far away from here."

She nodded and helped him to his feet. "What's your name?"

"I'm Aaron. Aaron Beine. I'm a freshman."

"Vickie Hewitt. Sophomore. I'm on the cross country team and we're down here for practice."

He turned his ear and leaned forward in an effort to hear over the rain. "Nice day for a run." He chuckled nervously. "Anyway, thanks. I should go. You need to get back to practice."

"Are you sure you're okay?" She noticed his slumped shoulders. He was still a little shocked by everything that had happened.

"I'll be fine." He put on a brave face like any freshman boy would do in front of a girl. "Thanks again. Go back to practice before you lose the rest of the team."

The vampire smiled. *That's not a problem.*

Once he had safely reached street level and she was sure he couldn't see her, she turned in the direction of the team and bolted until they were in sight about two seconds later. Undetected, she reverted to normal human speed and sprinted the rest of the way to catch up to them.

"There you are," Krista shouted at her when she approached. "Where were you?"

"I…um, I had to go to the bathroom quick. We're good."

They finished their run and returned to the school. In the entrance, they all stopped at the floor mats and scraped their shoes a few times in a futile effort to dry them. Despite several minutes of wiping them as best they could, the halls still echoed with the loud squeaks of wet running shoes on tile.

The soggy teams reunited in the classroom. A happily bone-dry Coach Lueck greeted them with a satisfied smile. "It looks like we all managed good miles today."

One by one, the teammates sat in desks and many of them immediately began to free their feet from their rain-soaked prisons, dropped mushy socks and shoes to the floor, and aired their wrinkled toes.

"Our first meet is only a week away, so for the rest of this week and next week, we'll pace out on the track. Here are your assignments for the first events…" The coach rattled off various team configurations and runner's assignments.

Vickie was assigned the 3200 and something called the four-by-four, although she didn't know what either of those meant.

Once in the locker room and in the process of peeling off the now heavy, wet layers of clothing, she stepped over to Krista, her voice low to avoid embarrassment. "I don't know what either of those races are. What is he talking about?"

"Oh, you're not familiar with track." Her friend nodded while she snatched a towel to dry herself. "The 3200 race is a two-miler. That's eight laps around the track. And then the four-by-four is a relay race where each of us will take one lap around the track. We'll decide which order we run in when we go out onto our track to practice the baton handoffs and stuff like that."

The vampire stared at her in astonishment. "The whole race is on the track?"

Krista laughed with disbelief. "That's why it's called track, Vickie. Yeah, all the races are on the track. You simply run in circles."

She returned to her locker to finish getting dressed. *Shoot. That means there will be people around. There's no place to hide like in cross country where I could relax in the woods or something. If someone trips my instincts, I will have to really keep them under control.*

When she thought of her instincts, her mind drifted to the poor boy who almost drowned. Having more control over them had been a wonderful thing, and she was happy that she could use them for good. *He would be dead by now if it wasn't for me.* She straightened and puffed her chest out a little.

Still, you know how to switch it on. If you run track, though, you'll have to know how to turn it off. Her shoulders slumped again as she sat down on the bench to put her shoes on.

Seeing her friend's nerves, Krista patted her on the back. "Don't worry about it. It's still only running. You'll do great once you get the hang of it."

Track isn't the only thing I need to get the hang of.

CHAPTER TWO

Craig wandered slowly in and out of the living room and the kitchen as he spoke on the phone.

"Uh huh…no kidding. Wow. I never thought about it like that. Yep, yep. Oh, I see what you mean, sure." He could barely hide the bored tone in his voice but it didn't matter. He obviously couldn't get much of a word in anyway.

In the living room, Alexis sprawled on the floor watching TV while Vickie swiped through her phone. The vampire watched Craig's multiple entrances and exits and shot her sister a confused look. "Does he have to do that?"

"Only when he's talking to someone annoying." Alexis shook her head. "If he's stuck in a conversation that he can't get out of, he gets anxious."

"Who's he talking to?"

"I have no idea."

"Okay, well I guess we'll see you soon then." Craig stopped at the entrance to the living room with a spooked expression. "That sounds good. You too. Bye." He ended the conversation, leaned his shoulder against the wall, and stared at the carpet while he cradled the phone in his hands. "Alexis…I have some news."

His daughter sat up straight with her eyes wide. The last time he'd used that tone of voice with her, he'd told her his mother passed away. Whatever this was, it was serious. "What is it?"

With a deep breath, he unleashed the news. "Your Aunt Renee is coming."

She curled her upper lip and tilted her head in disbelief. "Ugh. No. Really? Tell me you're joking."

He shook his head as he slid the phone into his pocket. "No, I'm not joking, even a little. She'll be here on Friday."

His daughter raised her eyebrows hopefully. "I work this weekend. Tell me she's staying here for the weekend. If it's only a couple days, I can deal with that."

"Not exactly."

Her stomach dropped. "A whole week with her? I don't know if I can handle that."

Craig deliberately avoided eye contact. "No…"

Alexis rose to her feet and folded her arms. "Tell me how long she's staying, Dad."

He lowered his voice until it was almost inaudible. "A month."

She stuck her finger in her ear and wiggled it around sarcastically. "I'm sorry, I must be losing my hearing. Did you say a month? A month? Please tell me you didn't actually say that and I'm going deaf because I would seriously be okay with that right now."

"Honey, I know she's difficult to handle, but she was your mother's only sister—"

"But what does she have to come here for? And stay for

a month? How is that fair? I can't live with that woman for a month."

Craig walked past her and sank into his recliner, defeated. "I couldn't say no to her."

"Then call her back. I'll do it."

Her chutzpah made him crack a smile. *Your mother would have had the same reaction.* "She's not only coming for fun. Aunt Renee will help me go through some of your mother's things and we both know that's long overdue."

Vickie straightened on the couch. "That sounds weird. Why would you want to go through all that stuff?"

Craig turned to his adopted daughter. "Because it's stacked up in the basement and on her side of the closet and she's not here anymore. It's what you do when someone passes away—you go through their stuff."

The vampire still didn't understand. "For what? What are you looking for?"

He shrugged while Alexis paced nervously. "Anything that's worth keeping and you throw out the rest of it," he explained. "It can be a long process but it needs to be done. Usually, family members will gather to do it because they'll want to keep some things that are special to them."

His daughter snapped her fingers. "Grandma!"

Vickie gave her a quizzical look. "Is keeping your grandmother up for debate?"

"No, she lives with my grandma." Alexis gave her father pleading eyes. "Tell me Grandma's coming too. Then at least we'll have her to act as a buffer."

"Grandma can't be away from home that long, kid. It's only Aunt Renee this time."

The vampire raised her hand. "I'm sorry, I guess I still

don't see what the big deal is. What's the problem with Aunt Renee?"

Father and daughter gave each other knowing glances as if each wanted the other one to speak first. Craig finally obliged. "My late wife's sister simply has a very…particular personality."

"She's a nosy, obnoxious, unbearable human being." Alexis displayed an almost-rude attitude that caught Vickie off-guard. "I can't stand her. I never could. But she always came with Grandma, and my mom was usually good about running interference so I wouldn't have to spend too much time with her."

"Now, please, let's not be disrespectful here." He gave his daughter a stern look. "She's still your aunt, even if your mother isn't here anymore. She deserves a little respect."

Alexis scoffed. "She never shows it to anyone else. Did you ever notice how, whenever we went there to visit, she put you to work? Like, you had to clean the gutters, mow the lawn, fix the fence—"

He raised his palm. "Yes, I'm aware of what happens when we go up there to visit. I'm not a particular fan of Aunt Renee, but she is who she is. What can I do, tell her she can't come over and help go through all Mom's stuff? Besides, I need someone to help me with it. That's a job I've put off for months."

"Where do they live?" Vickie had begun to get more curious about this story and the woman involved.

"Tomahawk, Wisconsin." Craig nodded. "It's a small town about a three-hour drive from here—maybe three-and-a-half. Carol's mother and sister moved there in the eighties. They live in a double-wide mobile home on a small patch of land—not much to it, but it's quiet."

"Yeah, they spend their time going to the bar and drinking." Alexis shook her head with disdain. "They don't do much of anything else. Except watch their stories."

"Stories?" The reference confused Vickie.

Craig hung his head and laughed quietly. "They watch soap operas during the day. They never got cable TV, so Renee uses a VCR to record shows on videotapes."

None of the words in that sentence made sense to Vickie, but she tried to ignore it and move on.

"When we'd go up there, Renee always shouted at us to not touch her VCR." Alexis walked over to the recliner and sat, mimicking her aunt. She sat straight and rocked to the left and right, her face in a permanent scowl. "Don't touch. I'm recording my stories."

"Gosh, we haven't been up there since your mom passed." Craig sported a half-smile as he thought about their times visiting up north. "It's crazy how time passes. I hated those visits, but there was something about the small town that I always enjoyed."

"Me too." Alexis had to concede that point. "I liked visiting Grandma. Plus, getting the ice cream from the old gas station on the corner was awesome." She turned to Vickie. "It's in the middle of nowhere. Literally. Like, Tomahawk is nowhere, and there's this intersection with nothing on it except a gas station on one corner. That gas station, for whatever reason, had the greatest, most delicious soft-serve ice cream ever. I loved going up in summer for that reason alone."

Craig straightened in his chair. "You're maybe too

young to remember this, but we went camping there too and camped on Grandma's land. She has a big yard. That was fun."

His daughter crossed her legs and slumped down. "Why can't we have the good memories? I love that stuff. But we have to also deal with Renee and all her garbage."

He grimaced apologetically and patted her on the knee. "Sweetheart, that's how life works. You take the good and the bad. Heck, think of your mother. I had her, but I also became family with her sister."

Vickie leaned forward on the couch. "What do I need to watch out for? How bad will this get? Is there anything I can do?"

"I doubt it." Alexis laughed. "No matter how well you prepare, Renee will find a way to intrude, annoy, and basically ruin whatever you have going."

Skeptical, the vampire glanced at Craig. She expected him to look amused but he appeared to agree with Alexis. "No woman could be that bad," she insisted.

"Well…look, she's a human being. Let's not forget that, okay?" He rested his elbows on his knees. "But she does have a particular type of personality. I can't overlook that. She's tough to deal with." Alexis was about to scoff and he extended his arm to quiet her. "But she is still family and we will treat her with respect. All we can do right now is deal with it. And she will be a great help to me. She knows more about your mom's stuff than I do."

"That woman needs a man or something." Alexis rested her head on her fist. "She is desperate for attention."

"Okay, but do you see the problem? She needs someone —I agree with you—but where would she ever find anyone? Not at the bar in Tomahawk. There's only, like, three thousand people who live there. And she hangs out with her seventy-year-old mother. Part of her behavior is her simply being lonely and not knowing how to interact with other people." He stood from his chair. "So let's enjoy the quiet right now and prepare ourselves. We can push through the next month and come out the other side in one piece. I know we can."

Once he walked out of the room, Vickie turned to Alexis in disbelief. "I really can't believe you are making such a big deal out of one woman being here. Even if she's really annoying, it's not like… Come on, she's only one person."

Her sister rubbed her temples. "You really won't understand what we're saying until she gets here. No matter how you approach it, this visit will suck—badly. Man, I wish Grandma was coming, at least. She's sweet. Aunt Renee is anything but sweet. She's not single because she lives in Tomahawk, trust me. I bet she was nowhere near getting a date when she lived in Milwaukee."

"A month seems like a really long time." Vickie knew she was stating the obvious but she was trying to at least get the focus off Renee personally. "Is it normal for someone to stay for a month like this?"

"Nope. But that's Renee. She merely wants to do whatever she feels like and doesn't care about how it impacts anyone else around her. I bet she'll be here for fifteen minutes and you'll already wonder how much longer you have left."

The vampire winced. "This is bringing out a really ugly side of you."

"Yeah, it is. But that woman has never shown anyone care or concern. She's probably here because my mom had something she thought she was entitled to and wants to get her hands on it. She's not here to help my dad, that's for sure. There's no way she would go out of her way to help anyone."

CHAPTER THREE

Jim Trembo clapped his hands and listened to the sound echo across the field. "It'll be a good day today, gentlemen. I can feel it in my bones."

The sun shone brightly overhead and blue sky stretched as far as the eye could see. Other than the faint sound of light traffic driving almost a mile away, everything was peaceful and quiet.

Two steps behind Jim, Pete Stabone struggled to trudge through the mud of the field. His feet sloshed and slopped through the thick muck that clung to the sides and bottoms of his shoes. "I hope the day gets better than this."

His colleague unleashed a hearty laugh. "You have to stay positive, Pete. Today, we get to do some real digging. This is what we've been waiting for."

On the outside, he projected an air of confidence in what they were doing and how they were going about it. He wanted the team to know that there was reason to believe they were on the cusp of something great. If they all believed, they would work harder and get more accomplished.

But on the inside, he was terrified. *Your entire career is riding on this turning into something. You don't have any more excuses. It's now or never.*

The constant weather-related delays had taken their toll on him and the entire crew. Pete stepped forward a little to catch up with his superior and talk to him.

"Look, the crew is starting to lose it." The man gestured behind them at the rest of the group, who all wore navy-blue jumpsuits. "Honestly, I know I am. I miss my wife and kids. Frank over there recently had a kid and he's been here for weeks upon weeks. What will it take before we can go home?"

The question lit a fire in Jim's stomach so hot, he thought smoke would waft out of his mouth when he opened it. He gritted his teeth and tried to take a quiet, deep breath before he answered. "This trip is very important. Besides, we let Frank go home and be with his wife when she went into labor. I'm not that cold. We have something in front of us that could potentially fundamentally change our military and our society. Now come on, let's stick together on this. It's not only my baby—it's yours too. This is the kind of thing that makes careers, and you guys will win as much as me."

That was only a half-truth, and he knew it. He couldn't promise anything close to that, and the press usually wasn't interested in the guys who did the grunt work. Simply because someone was on a dig didn't mean their lives changed much. He would get the praise, the media attention, and the accolades—all things he was looking forward to having after years of being the butt of the joke at the Agency.

This is my moment. Today, I'll find it. I can feel it.

As they traversed the field, Jim checked the GPS coordinates on his watch. "We don't have too much farther to walk. We'll be there soon and we can start digging. This soft ground will be really easy to carve through."

"Yeah, about that..." Pete raised his index finger. "Are you sure this ground will be able to be analyzed? It's so wet now. We've waited way too long for this." He lifted his foot to reveal half an inch of mud clinging to the side of his shoe. "With this much saturation, it has to affect the results."

Jim sighed. He had been between a rock and a hard place for weeks. He turned to face the group and stopped them all from moving forward. "How many of you are as doubtful as Pete is?" Of the half-dozen people in front of him, four raised their hands. The blood rushed to his face. "Guys, we didn't have too many options here. I know we're all from the East Coast, but apparently, Wisconsin weather isn't particularly cooperative. That's not something we could control. The best we could do was wait it out. That blizzard that struck here ground everything to a halt. We wouldn't have been able to dig through the frozen dirt even if we tried."

Pete shook his head. "And you really think now is a better time? I don't think we'll have much of a result. If anything was left behind that we could analyze, it's probably washed down."

Jim pointed at him. "Down doesn't mean out. This might make digging more complicated or we might have to dig deeper, but that doesn't mean there won't be anything here. Now we have our test kits and our digging equipment." After scanning the group, he locked eyes with his dispirited colleague. "And anyone who wants to focus on the negatives of this mission—why it won't work or why things will be tougher—you're welcome to go home. I'm not interested in working alongside anyone who doesn't believe in what we're doing. This is the absolute closest we've ever been to pinpointing supernatural activity here in the United States. I definitely won't give up, and I don't want any of you to, either."

He spun away and began to walk in the direction in which his watch pointed. Although they were reluctant, the other members of the group fell in line behind him.

Jim had locked in the GPS coordinates of the area early on. Due to the secretive nature of the mission, he didn't want to block off anything physically, which would only serve to draw attention to the site. Because it was in an open field and could not be hidden or disguised, he had to use whatever technology he had available to him to enable him to keep track of the site.

"Can I ask a question as long as it is not perceived as being too negative?" Pete had suddenly become wary of speaking up. "How do we know that the area hasn't been tampered with? This is a public area right up against a row of houses and some of them probably have kids living in them. I'm merely asking from a purely scientific viewpoint."

He nodded and chuckled, happy that his quick speech had the desired effect. "You'll see." He led the group past the GPS coordinates on his watch and instead, stopped several yards beyond it at the base of a low hill that surrounded the basin of the field.

"Uh, sir?" The other man looked around, confused. "This doesn't look like the right place."

"That's because it's not. Wait here." Jim climbed up the hill a few feet, stooped, and picked up a small black box. He turned and held it up to the group. "I've monitored this place with this camera. It senses movement, temperature, and records in 4K video. It beams the feed to my phone."

Pete put his hands on his hips and squinted into the sunlight. "You've watched this place the whole time?"

"Hey, I can't leave anything to chance." Jim walked down the hill and rejoined the group. "So trust me when I tell you, no one has tampered with the site. Besides, this isn't the kind of field that kids run around in. It's basically the bottom of a lake. I had a feeling that everything would be fine but at least I had this little gadget to confirm my assumptions."

He led the team to the site while following the directions on his watch. Once they reached it, he looked at Pete and nodded.

The man nodded in response. "Okay, men. We'll dig through, one layer of dirt—or mud—at a time. Let's be patient and have the testing kits ready. I'll set the scanner up."

As they stepped forward to begin their work, he dropped a black briefcase he had carried onto the mud and opened it. He extended two tripods and positioned them in the dirt next to each other, lifted a wide metal box to rest on top of the tripods, and sank the supports deeper into the mud. On one end of the box was a lens that he faced in the direction of the area where they would dig.

Pete flipped a small switch on the back of the box and a green light beamed out of the lens and projected a grid of light ahead. After turning a few knobs to calibrate the size of the area and how it would scan, he gave his superior a thumbs-up.

"I hope this thing works." Jim smiled. "And it'll detect anything?"

"Any foreign substance," he corrected him. "I have everything punched into the system so it knows what we're looking for and what to ignore. Once anything is detected, that square or squares of the grid will turn from green to red and we can test from there."

The group fell to their knees and began to work, doing their best to cut through the muck without sabotaging the area or taking too much of it at once.

After almost an hour, they had worked consistently and nothing on the scanner had triggered red. Jim pushed himself into a seated position and the mud had painted his jumpsuit mostly brown. "This is my favorite and my least favorite part of the job."

Pete took a break as well to catch his breath. "Why do you say that?"

"I hate the digging. But the fact that we're digging is a good sign. It means we're making progress. And I know it will be worth it, but I also wonder when that will be. Because right now? I'm exhausted and have nothing to show for it."

"Hang in there." His companion slapped him on the shoulder. "This is like archaeology. It is archaeology, I guess. Digs take a long time. It's about being patient. It may not be the most exciting thing in the world, but if everything you've said is true and you can be confident that whatever is here is still here, this will pay off."

They persisted for several hours and meticulously carved away layer after layer in an effort to reveal anything they could connect to the sword they had already retrieved from the area.

Finally, after nearly four hours of digging, two squares on the green grid blinked red.

Pete was ecstatic. "We have something! Grab the test kits and let's take a sample." He opened one of the kits and scooped a little dirt from the red area. After placing it in a glass beaker, he poured a chemical solution over the top and swirled it. The mixture turned a bright blue. He smiled.

"What does that mean?" Jim shook his head.

"It means we've found blood, Jim."

Trembo pumped his fist in excitement. "What kind of blood? Can we tell?"

"Not with this test. It's merely a broad test of substances. We can load this up, take a little more from the area, and get it to Washington's lab for further testing."

Without much deliberation or discussion, that was exactly what they did. Once they took a sizable sample from that area, they dug for a few more hours and uncovered two more places with blood and gathered samples they could take with them.

Once they were finished, the two colleagues looked at the area with awe. Jim couldn't stop smiling. "It's such a small patch of land, but the information in here could completely change our lives and careers."

Pete elbowed him in the ribs. "I told you it would pay off."

"You were right."

"We both were. Now, let's get out of here. I need a shower."

CHAPTER FOUR

Vickie and Eric walked hand in hand along the parking lot in front of the Pettit National Ice Center.

She raised an eyebrow. "We're not going for a run, are we?"

"That wouldn't be much of a date, would it?" He laughed. "I think I prefer a little less puking on my dates."

They both chuckled and gazed at the large neon sign that hung over the entrance. It displayed a United States flag with the words *US OLYMPIC TRAINING SITE* across the length of the building.

"I don't remember that sign being there." She would remember something like that if she'd seen it.

"Me neither. It must be new. But it looks cool." He stepped forward to open the door for her. "You know, it's a good reminder, too. Like, you don't think about Milwaukee being the home of anything all that important. The sign points out that some things here are still a big deal."

They walked into the lobby of the Pettit Center and directly to the counter where they could rent ice skates. After they each got a pair, they walked through the giant metal doors leading to the track and the ice rink.

"It'll be nice to be here when I'm not dreading it." Eric shook his head. "I don't even know what's it like to be here without having to run the track."

"I haven't even been ice skating before," Vickie admitted.

"Really?" He sat on a bench outside the railing and kicked his shoes off. "Your family never goes ice skating?"

She tilted her head. "Not together. Alexis went a few months ago, but that went poorly." Vickie was referring to her date with Will, a relationship that ultimately ended with the boy trying to eat her flesh—about as bad as any relationship could go.

"Stick with me. You'll be fine out there." He leaned over and bumped her shoulder as he tied his skates.

She blushed and smiled warmly. "That's my plan." When she puckered her lips, he obliged and planted a long kiss on her before he stood and helped her to waddle to the entrance.

Once on the ice, her feet almost immediately slid out from under her and she sprawled on the ice. Her instincts kicked in and she was able to catch herself with her hands before her butt made contact. The hair on the back of her neck stood up, and she quickly became aware of her surroundings.

"Whoops! Are you okay?" Eric took her by the hand and helped her to her feet.

"I'm fine." She brushed herself off. "I wasn't expecting that. I'm sorry."

"It's nothing to be sorry for." While he held her hand, he pushed forward, glided on the ice, and showed her how it was done. He made it look effortless.

His comfort on the ice actually reassured her, and she settled into skating rather quickly. Because her senses were so heightened by that point, she could immediately note the subtleties of every motion and instantly apply what she learned.

After only a minute or two of observation, she relaxed and was able to skate as well as him. He was impressed. "I've never seen someone learn to skate so quickly. Nice work. See? You should have been on the ice this whole time."

The rink was not terribly crowded. Several mothers had brought their children to skate. Some joined their offspring to skate around and help them learn. Others simply sat on the benches outside the rink and stared at their phones.

The more Vickie skated, the more confidence she built up in herself. Eric had skated for years, so he knew all the tricks. He threw in a few spins and circled her as they moved around the ice. Once in a while, he moved backward in front of her, which made her laugh—and gave her a chance to stare into his eyes for a few seconds.

Soon, she was able to do as many tricks as he could. He almost fell over when she skated backward in front of him.

"You look surprised." She flashed him a knowing grin.

"I am! I've been doing this for years. It took me a long

time to work up to skating backward, and you're doing it flawlessly on your first attempt."

"I guess I'm a fast learner." She winked at him, which sent chills down his spine. Something about her sent shockwaves through his body whenever she did little flirty things like that.

They skated onward and moved carefully to avoid the slower little kids, who flopped and slipped around them. Eric took Vickie by the hand and squeezed it.

This is a great opportunity to do it, man. But what if she doesn't say anything? Or what if you freak her out? Come on, how difficult can it be? Tell her how you feel. Girls love hearing that. You mean it, so why don't you just say it? Dude, look at her. She's smiling at you, winking at you, holding your hand. She loves being here. Just say it.

She sighed. "This is so much fun. I had no idea. I love ice skating."

His voice cracked with nerves. "I love…ice skating too. It's fun, isn't it?" They shared a smile.

You wimp. What are you so afraid of? She's won't break up with you because you say it. Or would she? Is that moving too fast? You've dated for months. What's the harm?

Sweat began to form on his brow and his hands grew clammy. "Hey, uh…I need to go to the restroom for a second. Excuse me." He skated to the exit of the rink, where he could step off the ice and waddle over to the bathroom.

She drew her eyebrows together in a small frown. *Hmm. He's nervous. Something is really unsettling him. I wonder what it is. I hope it's not me. I'm not doing anything. Or I'm not trying to, anyway. I hope he feels better soon. He's much more fun when he's not so nervous.*

The hair on the back of her neck stood up again. Blood rushed through her veins. Something was happening.

She scanned the area and saw a little girl of about four years old hurtle down the ice faster than almost every other kid at the rink that day. She had clearly lost control, and the vampire could sense that she was in immediate danger.

But while other children were content to merely flop to the ice, this child stayed on her feet while she rushed toward the wall of the rink.

The vampire had to think quickly. *If she collides into the wall at that speed, she could be seriously hurt.* She looked around at who was watching. *Only a few kids would see me. The parents aren't paying attention and I'll move faster than anyone could notice anyway. Do it.*

She gritted her teeth and burst across the ice with as much speed as she could muster on such short notice. When she reached the youngster, she grasped her by the arms and stopped her within a few feet of the side wall.

"You really need to be a little more careful, sweetheart." She stroked the girl's hair to comfort her. The little one thanked her between sobs before she scurried away to leave the rink.

A satisfied Vickie turned as large flakes of what appeared to be snow fell from above. At first, she wondered if that was even possible. But when she glanced at the ice, she noticed why they were falling.

A long, deep crevice had been carved into the surface by her skates. Because she'd moved so quickly, her blades dug into the ice and scored it deeply to hurl the resulting ice chips and flakes upward.

A few of the kids on the ice began to cheer, as they had seen everything that happened. None of the parents had bothered to watch, so they missed the entire situation.

Once the vampire had calmed, she circled the rink and reached the exit where Eric stood. "I'm hungry. Do you want me to get us some food?" He pointed to the quick-service counter behind him. She agreed and stepped off the ice to sit on a bench.

Minutes later, he joined her with a couple of sodas, two hot dogs, and two bags of chips. "It's not the most nutritious meal, but at least it's something," he joked.

The lack of nutrition didn't bother her and she scarfed her hot dog in only a few bites before she ripped her chips open and began to shovel them into her mouth.

Eric laughed while he watched her eat so ravenously. It wasn't the most attractive look for her, but he didn't mind. In fact, he loved to watch her no matter what she did.

He merely couldn't admit it out loud.

"Are you hungry today?"

"Oh, man, I'm so hungry." She spoke between mouthfuls. "I don't know why, but in the last couple of days, I've been really starving. I guess you could say I've worked up quite an appetite."

Without hesitation, he handed her the rest of his hot dog. He had eaten only half of it but she needed it more than him. With little in the way of manners, she snatched up the half and shoved the entire thing in her mouth.

Still, her stomach rumbled.

"Let me go get you some more." He stood from the

bench.

Despite her protests, he returned with another hot dog and a large hot pretzel with melted cheese. She tore into both with eagerness in an effort to assuage the hunger that plagued her.

Now's definitely not the time, Eric. Wait for a little while until she feels more comfortable. Maybe you can muster up a little confidence in the meantime.

Defeated by his own cowardice, Eric took Vickie out on the ice to enjoy what was left of their date. Several kids pointed and stared at her, as some of them had witnessed her super-speed with their own eyes, although their parents wouldn't believe it.

She heard them whining and smiled inwardly.

"That's her!"

"You have to believe me!"

"She was so fast I couldn't even see her!"

All their parents, no doubt weary of exaggerated stories over the years from their children, smiled and nodded politely and brushed off any of their claims as being ridiculous and unrealistic.

Little did they know that, had they looked up from their phones, they would have seen it for themselves.

As they skated across the deep cut that she had accidentally carved in the ice, Eric was stunned. "Holy cow, who did this? That's crazy. They'll need to put in a fair amount work to smooth this out. I've never seen such a trench dug in there."

She simply played dumb, took her boyfriend's hand, and smiled at him to distract him.

Fortunately, it worked.

CHAPTER FIVE

"Why do I have to do this again?" Vickie grumbled while she pulled a stack of shirts out of the top drawer of her dresser and stuffed them into a suitcase.

Craig sighed from the doorway to her bedroom. "Because this is where Aunt Renee stays when she's here. And since you're in this room now, you'll have to move to the basement for the month."

She straightened and stretched her back. "And that means I have to live out of a suitcase for an entire month, too? I have to walk past this room on the way to the shower in the morning anyway. Why can't I grab my clothes then?"

He chuckled at the thought but before he could respond, his daughter poked her head in. "Yeah. The woman who won't let you touch her thirty-year-old VCR will let you walk into her bedroom to get clothes every day. Go ahead and see how that works out for you."

"I'd let you stay in Alexis' room, but her waterbed is so big, you wouldn't have any space on the floor to sleep.

You'd have to share a bed for a month, and I doubt you want to do that."

"Heck no!" Alexis looked at her father. "Hey, Vickie, at least there's a pullout couch down there. It's not so bad. I've slept on it before."

The vampire didn't respond. She was still annoyed that she had to pack and move her life around because a visitor decided to practically move in with them.

"We'll do our best to keep everyone comfortable." Craig leaned against the door frame and put his hands in his pockets. "As comfortable as any of us can be, anyway."

"Why can't she stay in the basement?" Vickie suggested. "She can have the whole space to herself. There's tons of room. And it would be easier on all of us, right?"

He knew that she didn't understand what they were talking about. "You'll see when she gets here. That arrangement wouldn't work for a variety of reasons. And if we want any chance at even a little peace over the next month, we'd be smart to make her as comfortable as possible."

As the girl zipped her suitcase, he walked into the kitchen and looked out the window at the field behind the house. In the far distance, he could make out a hole that had been dug and which appeared, even from where he stood, to be fairly deep. *Either someone's building a fort or they're looking for something out there. Goodness.*

Alexis walked into Vickie's room and threw her arm around her shoulders. "I know this seems bad. But actually, this is a good arrangement for you. Hey, you get the whole basement. Besides, Aunt Renee snores like a pig with sleep apnea. Me and my dad's only hope for a good night's sleep will be to get to bed before her and fall asleep before the snoring starts. You'll be a good distance away from her."

Ding-dong.

The three of them all held their breaths as they looked in the direction of the side door of the house. Craig ran his fingers through his hair. *No more avoiding it. Time to face the music.*

He paused with his hand on the doorknob and tried to psych himself up for the coming visitor. After a deep breath that did little to calm him, he turned the knob and pulled the door open. "Hi, Renee."

"Craig," she blurted in an obnoxiously loud voice.

Hiding his grimace, he pushed the screen door open. She grasped one side of the door frame, placed one foot into the house, and pulled with her arms to hoist herself through the door and inside. She grunted loudly, panting because she was out of breath already. "Woo! It feels like these steps get higher and higher every time I come here."

He let that comment go as he pressed his body up against the interior door and shoved it against the wall behind him to make room for Renee to squeeze through.

She shuffled her feet into the kitchen. When she heard her, Alexis strolled from her room into Vickie's. "It's show-time. Are you ready?"

The vampire stared morosely at her suitcase where its contents strained the metal teeth of the zipper. She nodded bleakly. "I guess so."

The two girls walked into the kitchen where a smiling Aunt Renee was waiting to greet them.

Vickie immediately noted the unique appearance of the woman. She was shorter than her by a couple of inches but appeared to weigh in excess of two hundred and fifty pounds. Her stubby legs poked out from under a long, flowing pink blouse, and her feet were wedged into a cheap pair of flip-flops.

Unnaturally curly hair adorned her head, the result of a cheap perm that cinched her hair so it only touched halfway down the back of her neck. It was a mixture of dark-brown and gray.

The vampire was surprised. Alexis described her mother in friendly terms—as though they hung out together often. She seemed to be full of energy and youthfulness. But this woman before them was slow, overweight, and not particularly well-kept. *She must be an older sister or something. She looks nothing like the pictures of Alexis' mom.*

Renee extended her arms dramatically to welcome Alexis in for a big bear hug. She pressed her niece tightly against her chest and pushed the side of her head awkwardly into her bosom. "My dear, dear Alexis." She practically wailed over the girl. "How are you holding up, my little flower?"

The girl closed her eyes tightly and did her best to let it happen. Fighting it would do her no good. "I'm good, Aunt Renee. It's nice to see you." Her tone was far from convincing.

"Oh, I'm sure you're doing your best. You poor girl. Let me get a look at you." She pushed her back by her shoulders and cupped her cheeks with her hands, leaned forward, and shook her head slightly. "You are growing like a weed. My gosh! And looking more and more like your mother every day." She released the girl's face and covered her mouth with her hand. "I'm so sorry, dear. I didn't mean to bring it up."

Alexis gave her a polite smile. "It's okay, Aunt Renee. We still talk about my mom."

She shook her head with what could have been a tear in her eye, although its sincerity might be in question. "You are so brave. Your mother would be proud of you. And Craig." She waddled to the side to let him into the kitchen, although he hadn't exactly tried to force his way in. She wrapped him in a hug as well, but he made sure that his arms were on top of hers to avoid getting pulled too close. "Oh! It's so good to see you. Thank you for letting me come down and stay with you for a little while."

"We're happy to have you, Renee." *Not that you gave us much of a choice.*

Renee turned her head to see Vickie standing politely behind the others. "Is this a friend of yours, dear?"

Alexis froze for a second. In all their preparations, they had never really discussed how they would explain her presence.

Craig thought quickly. "This is a girl from Alexis' school. She's a transfer student staying with us for now. She's from Austria and her name is Vickie."

Renee extended a polite hand and spoke loudly and slowly. "It is very nice to meet you. Welcome to America."

The vampire looked puzzled and turned to her sister. "What is she doing?"

Alexis smirked in response. "She thinks you can't speak English."

She nodded and shook Renee's hand. "Thank you, but I

can speak English fine. I love America, and I am enjoying my stay with the family here."

The woman placed a hand on her chest and shook her head. "Such a sweetheart. And very well said." Her head snapped to her left, looking at the door. "Oh! I forgot to bring Lucky in. Craig, could you be a dear…"

He heaved an inward sigh. "Of course."

While her aunt wasn't looking, Alexis twisted her face in annoyance when she heard the name Lucky. When the little poodle hopped into the house from outside, he immediately began to yip and bark infuriatingly.

"Awww." Vickie crouched to welcome him into the house. The dog's tight black curly hair almost reminded her of Renee's hair to an extent. He appeared to have unlimited energy, hopped on his hind legs, and howled weakly. When she reached out to pet him, he yipped and bit her on the hand.

"Lucky! No!" Renee swatted her hand at the dog, although it came nowhere near him. The animal backed away but continued to howl at Vickie, who gave up and straightened.

"I guess I'd better take my bag and head to the basement so you can unpack." She began to walk back to her room.

"She is a sweet girl." The woman shook her head again. "You really got a nice one there, Craig. My friend Nancy Sullivan took in a foreign exchange student a few years ago. She spent six months stealing from her and even took her wedding ring. All she did was stay in her room all the time, not talking to anyone, and stealing from under their noses."

Craig placed his hand on her shoulder. "I wouldn't

worry too much about that happening here, Renee. Vickie is basically a member of the family by this point." He winked at Alexis, who smiled in response. He leaned back a little to create some distance between himself and Renee without being rude—the overpowering odor of cigarette smoke had begun to irritate him.

Vickie emerged from the hallway, dragging her suitcase. Renee looked confused. "Wait, why aren't you sleeping with Alexis in her room?"

The girls looked at each other but he jumped in first. "We thought it was best that everyone have their own space, that's all. Vickie says it's no problem to sleep in the basement for a few weeks. You know how teenage girls are."

"Ugh." Renee sneered. "That reminds me of my cousin Cheryl. She grew up with eight other kids in a three-bedroom house. She shared a twin bed with her sister Geri until they were out of high school. Can you imagine?"

No one said anything, and the woman walked through the kitchen while Vickie made her way to the basement.

As she walked, she called over her shoulder. "Craig, can you give me a hand with my bags? They're in the trunk."

And by that, you're asking me to bring in your bags. "No problem, Renee."

Once the woman reached the middle bedroom, she was in awe. "Would you look at this place? My goodness. The TV is huge."

"Oh, yeah, that's Vickie's." Alexis peeked in from the hall. "She bought it a while ago."

"It's like you people don't even want me to leave." Renee

let out a belly laugh, plopped herself down on the edge of the bed, and sighed loudly as Lucky nipped at her feet.

Don't even joke about that. Alexis removed herself quickly from the situation before she blurted anything out.

At the other end of the house, Craig lugged two over-packed suitcases into the side door. *It's only a month. It's only a month. It's only a month...*

CHAPTER SIX

Seventh-period study hall was always a powder keg waiting to explode.

It was held in one of the German classrooms, which was ironically located in the English Hall. The desks were old and wooden, some seats were loose, and it was consistently too hot to do anything.

Because it was the seventh period, there was only one more class after it before the end of the school day. As such, the students were usually restless. While they did their best to keep it together, they were anxious to end the misery of school for another evening.

It didn't help that Mr Schumacher, the teacher in charge of the study hall, was already exhausted by that point in the day. Once attendance was taken, he routinely folded his arms on his chest, leaned back in his chair, and fell soundly asleep for the duration of the period. Other than his long mustache shaking every time he exhaled, he didn't move at all.

This led most of the students to reorganize themselves after he nodded off. On one side of the room, toward the back, Megan and Abby sat beside one another to joke, gossip, and talk trash about the other kids. On the other end of the room, in the front row near the door, Vickie tried to make the best of study hall and get some work done.

On that day, the two troublemakers had no interest in doing homework—not that they usually did, anyway. Once they took their seats, Megan tapped her foot restlessly.

"What's your deal?" Abby asked and nodded to her foot.

"I have an idea I want to run by you." Her friend peered over her shoulder at Vickie to make sure she wasn't paying attention. "I want to set Vickie up."

The other girl was dumbfounded. "Seriously? With who?"

She closed her eyes and shook her head. "No, not on a date. Really? You think I want to set her up on a date?"

"That's why I was confused." Abby giggled. "Besides, she has a boyfriend."

"Yeah, well, there's no one I hate that much anyway. No, I have a plan. I want to set Vickie up to get in trouble."

"Ooh…" The girl leaned in with a raised eyebrow. "Now we're talking. What do you want to do? Make her miss a class or something?"

"Better. I want everyone to think that Vickie beat me up." She wore a satisfied smile on her face, confident that this was a brilliant plan.

Abby wasn't convinced. "I…don't know how you can do that. Like, will you pick a fight with her?"

In her mind, Megan wondered why she had to be

friends with someone so dumb. "Abby, come on. Obviously, I don't want her to actually beat me up. I want people to think she did. I make it look like I was beaten up and I blame her."

The thought of carrying this out made the girl squirm in her seat. "I don't know. Don't you think that's a little too far? People get arrested for beating other people up. You could really do some damage here."

Her friend muffled her laughter. "Oh, my gosh, can you imagine if I got her arrested? That would be hilarious. But no, it's not like I want anyone to think she inflicted serious injury on me. Only some bruises or something. If she gets arrested, we risk getting in trouble for misleading the cops or whatever. I don't want that."

As she leaned back, Abby tried to make sense of this idea that was sprung so suddenly upon her. "How long have you been thinking about doing this?"

Megan shrugged. "A while, I guess."

"And why go so far?"

"Come on. The girl humiliates us at every turn. She gets one up on us whenever we try to do something to her. I'm tired of it. I want to go nuclear. One last push, once and for all. I want to get her suspended or something."

Abby raised her eyebrows. "If she gets busted for beating someone up, she could even be expelled."

"Even better." She stuck her bottom lip out. "It doesn't bother me any."

"That's serious business." The other girl experienced the slightest twinge of conscience. "It wouldn't bother you if you were responsible for doing that to someone?"

"Nope." Megan shook her head. "Think about what

school was like before she got here. We had fun and we ran the place. Now, we have to be all careful to not cross her. I'm tired of it. I want to get back to the way things used to be."

Her friend nodded. She was right. Things were much more fun before Vickie came to the school and foiled them every time they tried to embarrass her. The girls liked to have that control and wield it over people. The newcomer had made them a little more powerless, and the frustration was a constant irritant. "Okay, what do you need from me?"

"I only need a witness." Megan took a moment to think this through. "Someone who can vouch for my story. It doesn't have to be much, obviously. I can do all the lying. All you have to do is say I'm telling the truth."

Abby didn't mind being the witness. If the truth be told, she actually enjoyed the idea. She'd gathered from the shows she watched that witnesses were important. But she also wondered if her friend had maybe gone a little crazy. *She's really thought this through. How badly is Vickie bothering her that she is willing to go through all this nonsense to get her in trouble?*

"So will you beat yourself up, then? How does this even work?" She imagined the other girl alone in the girls' bathroom throwing punches at herself while looking in the mirror.

"I don't need to go that far. All I need is well-applied makeup, nothing more. That will make it look like I've taken a few punches from her. We could create a little reddish-purple on my cheekbone for a bruise, and maybe give me a black eye—if we can make it look convincing." That confirmed her suspicions—Megan had really thought this through.

She looked across the room at Vickie, who was quietly doing her homework. "You're not going to need, like, a doctor's note or anything?"

Megan stared past her for a moment, deep in thought. "I think we can get away without one. If it's only bruising, we wouldn't need to go to the doctor for that. But if they require a note from a doctor, we can put something together that looks legit."

"I still feel like it's missing something." She rested her head on her hand and tilted it to the side while her mind considered the scenario. "It's not convincing enough to me. If we actually do this, we have to go all the way with it, you know? Because the first question they'll ask her is why she would do this. If they can't establish some kind of motive, it's won't be believable."

Her friend muffled a giggle that sounded smug. "Now you're getting into this. You sound like a detective on some TV show."

Abby didn't laugh. "Hey, I'm trying to cover all the bases here. They'll ask that kind of stuff, won't they? We need to be prepared. Actually, they'll probably ask you first why she would do that. So, you need a story."

At that Megan, straightened to stretch her back and turned her attention to Vickie in the front row. Her target sat closest to the door of the classroom and the waste-basket stood on the floor beside it. She turned to her friend. "I think I have an idea. And this will be good because it'll set her off in front of a group of other people. Watch."

Her grin wide, she dug in her backpack and located a bottle of water she had purchased in the cafeteria that day. It was about half-full, which was all she needed. She stood from the desk and unscrewed the cap.

Trying her best to look natural, she sauntered to the front of the classroom and headed to the wastebasket. Once she was within a few steps of Vickie, she made sure Mr Schumacher was still asleep and that no one else was looking at her.

In that perfect moment, she poured the water all over the girl's desk. Her homework, her textbooks, and even her pants were all drenched by the spill.

Vickie uttered a loud gasp, not prepared for the cold water on the front of her pants. But more crucially for Megan, her homework was waterlogged, which would force her to start over again. That was a wonderful bonus, come to think of it.

"What are you doing?" she shouted as she leapt from her chair. "You've ruined my homework."

"Oh, golly, I'm so sorry, Vickie." Megan put on the performance of a lifetime. "I tripped when I was walking to the wastebasket. I was finishing my water and—ooh, that doesn't look good. Oops."

The girl stepped forward so forcefully that she wondered briefly if she wouldn't throw a punch anyway. The plan was working—and possibly a little too well.

When she had gasped, Mr Schumacher jumped up violently and shook the grogginess off to see what all the commotion was about.

Both girls were immediately questioned about what had happened. Vickie claimed that Megan did it on purpose and made comments about how mad she was at the school for allowing this to happen. Megan played dumb and innocent and insisted that she tripped and it was a huge misunderstanding.

Because Mr Schumacher didn't want to fill out the paperwork associated with this kind of scenario, he tried to calm everyone down.

A buzz rippled through the classroom as various students leaned forward in their seats, expecting a fight to break out. From the back of the room, Abby smiled. She was impressed that her friend was able to make an entire room of students believe that their victim was ready to snap.

Once things settled, Megan ran and retrieved paper towels to clean the water on the desktop, floor, and the chair. When she had finished, she walked back to her desk, confident that the seed had been planted.

"That may have gone better than even I could have hoped for." She gave her friend a devilish smile. "For a second there, I actually thought I wouldn't have to make anything up and that she would actually beat me up right then and there."

Abby shook her head. "I was here and I thought for sure she would deck you. I'm kinda impressed she didn't."

"But Abby, she did punch me." She was already practicing their cover for the incident. "Didn't you see it?"

The other girl nodded slowly. "Ah yes. I'm surprised she didn't kill you. That girl has a much shorter fuse than anyone seems to realize."

"And it's only a matter of time until it takes her down." Megan spun to face forward, folded her arms, and stared at her adversary, who was still fuming about the entire incident.

CHAPTER SEVEN

After study hall was over, Vickie noticed several of her fellow students watching her walk out of the room.

She was steaming mad. Not only had her homework been ruined and she'd have to start over again, but the front of her pants was soaking wet. Much like the infamous bubbler ride that high school students liked to prank each other with, the girl's little stunt had left her appearing as though she'd had some kind of embarrassing accident.

With her *World History* textbook clutched in one hand, she tried to cover the front of her pants while still looking casual. *That girl really makes me want to kill her some days.*

Through gritted teeth, she took a few deep breaths. If she got worked up, she would have trouble concentrating on her eighth-period world history class. Before she headed to the other side of the school building, however, she turned right out of the room and stopped at her locker, which was located immediately next to the door.

I think I still have a sweatshirt tucked away in here some-

where. Maybe I can tie that around my waist and make it look a little less humiliating.

She popped her locker open and saw a note folded into a small triangle and taped to the edge of the top shelf. Dangling in front of her, it simply had *Vickie* scrawled across it.

It must be a note from Eric. Vickie smiled for a moment as she pulled the note off the shelf and tucked it into her pocket. She had recently given him the combination to her locker and once in a while, he liked to leave little notes inside for her as a surprise.

He had quickly become one of her favorite things about high school. Their relationship was going smoothly and they were crazy about each other and had tremendous fun to boot. These little notes were merely another benefit of having a boyfriend.

She stuck her head into her locker and moved a few books and a duffel bag aside until she saw the light-gray color of her sweatshirt peeking out through the mess. A good yank was sufficient to pull it out of the locker and she kicked the door shut.

With a heavy sigh, she tied the arms of the sweatshirt around her waist so the body portion hung in front of her like a skirt. It was not at all natural and looked very obvious that she was hiding something, but it was better than walking around with wet pants.

Aside from that, she might pass as a billboard for the Green Bay Packers football team, she thought waspishly. The front of the sweatshirt displayed a large yellow football helmet with the green-and-white *G* on it, and the words *GREEN BAY PACKERS* in all-caps surrounding it.

In Wisconsin, such a loud image was viewed as a good thing, anyway.

As she made her way through the halls to her history class, she remembered the note in her pocket. She fumbled for it and pulled it out to unfold carefully while she walked.

I wonder what it will be this time? Something about how he's thinking of me? Or that he can't wait to see me? That boy knows the right things to say to make me melt. He's so sweet.

But to her surprise, the note had nothing of the sort. It was one simple sentence with no hearts, smiley faces, or any other lighthearted doodles on it:

Meet me in the Band Hall after school right away.

This confused her. *Why would I meet him right away? He knows there's track practice after school that I have to get to. I don't have time to sit and talk. Wait...is that why he wants to meet me right away after school? What does he want to talk about? If it has to be fast, is that a good thing or a bad thing? Is he breaking up with me?*

Vickie was struck by the one massive drawback to dating in high school—the fear of the breakup.

Distracted, she crumpled the note and shoved into her pocket. Her mind raced while she walked through the halls and tried to make sense of the request.

Did I do something wrong? Is there someone else? Is he cheating on me? No, he wouldn't do that. He is too sweet a guy. Or, at least, that's what I think. Maybe I'm wrong. Maybe he does want to break up with me. What if he's tired of me? Am I not showing him enough attention?

The questions continued to pile up in her mind, and she did her best to try to shake them off, but there was no point. The message was cryptic enough to completely consume her.

While she walked to history, she saw Jess on the other side of the hallway, heading in the opposite direction.

"Jess!" She waved her hand and pushed her way past a few students to reach her.

"Hey, Vickie." The girl showed no indication that she knew anything about Eric's odd behavior. "What's up? I gotta get to family living class."

"I'll be really quick," she assured her. "Have you talked to Eric at all today?"

"A few times." She appeared confused by the question. "Why? What's going on?"

"Did he seem weird to you? Like, was anything off? Or something wrong? Or did he say anything to you about me?" She felt silly asking so many questions, but this was her only chance before the eighth period would begin.

Jess shook her head slowly. "Nope. He seemed fine to me. He didn't say anything. Are you okay?"

"I don't know. I think I'm fine, I guess." Honestly, Vickie didn't even know herself.

"Okay, I'll see you later."

"See ya."

That was all she could get. The bell would ring at any moment and she needed to be in her history class. No one else in that class would know anything, so she was stuck having to worry about it instead.

She sat there, dazed and confused, throughout the entire eighth period. While Mr Leverence stroked his dark beard and lectured the class on the history of ancient

Mesopotamia, she stared off into the distance, completely and utterly distracted.

The vampire had no idea what the teacher talked about. While she saw the diagrams of bordering countries, they didn't register to her. She would have been relieved, had she noticed, that he didn't call on her to answer any questions.

All she could think about was the note burning a hole in her pocket. *Why would we meet in the Band Hall? Why not at my locker? Or his locker? We see each other after school every single day. Why change that?*

At least the Band Hall made sense. Eric played the French horn in the band, so he had a locker there. He often hung out there with his band friends, much like Vickie hung out in the library at times.

But they rarely hung out in the Band Hall together. And they never made a point of meeting there. He didn't always like his band friends being around him and his girlfriend, so he avoided it—which added to her confusion.

At the same time, she felt very strange. Her stomach felt heavy but not twisted like it would be if she were scared or her powers were kicking in. Despite the discomfort, she was aware of her surroundings and when she ran her tongue along her teeth, no fangs poked out. She didn't feel as though she should run at the height of her speed.

Vickie felt normal, but her nerves were off-kilter.

I'm not in any physical danger or I'd be able to sense every-thing around me. I don't know what this is, but I don't like it.

As the clock ticked its way toward 3:00 pm, she shoved her books in her backpack, ready to escape as soon as the bell rang. It had no sooner sounded when she bounded to her feet and power-walked out of the room, the first one to the door. A few of her fellow students were taken aback by how quickly she exited.

"Geez, Vickie, what's your deal?"

"Are you late for something or what?"

She ignored the comments, bolted past everyone, and hurried to the Band Hall. The area was tucked away near the back of the school building. A long, windowless and doorless hallway stretched out in front of her, both cinderblock walls painted white on either side of her for maximum blandness.

The only break in the hallway was the faculty elevator door on her left—a curious addition to the school since no one had ever seen any member of the staff use it.

The end of the empty hallway opened into another section of the school, with back hallways and more banks of lockers. And, of course, the double doors opening into the Band Hall.

It had never looked bigger or more intimidating to her than in that moment. The large, cavernous room had acoustic panels mounted everywhere to dull the noise emptying out into the hallway and to improve the sound of the instruments within the space.

Immediately to her right and inside the entrance stood a small stack of beige lockers for band members to keep important belongings and besides those, a mishmash of various instruments, chairs, and music stands were scattered about in the open room.

On the far end of the room, a large window peeked into the Band Director's office. Mr Mannisto, the director, hunched over his desk and worked on something. His bald head reflected light out into the room.

Next to his office was a short hallway with several tiny practice rooms where students could work on their craft without being disturbed.

To Vickie's dismay, Eric had not arrived there yet. She was stuck waiting for several minutes and tapped her foot nervously.

A nerdy blond boy approached her with a friendly smile on his face. Steve Kopitzke was a nice enough guy, but she was totally horrified to see him. *Great, here comes Steve. He's the last thing I need right now. The boy doesn't know how to read people even a little. I've only been here a year and I can understand social cues better than him.*

"Hey, Vickie!" He spoke with a nasal voice. Steve wore his usual uniform of t-shirt with sleeves entirely too short for him and which exposed the maximum amount of his pasty white arms. Although he played the tuba—a large instrument—his arms looked like he couldn't hold a flute for more than a few seconds before tiring. The cuffs of his ill-fitting jeans missed the top of his shoes by three or four inches and bared his tube socks for the world to see.

"Hi, Steve."

"Are you waiting for Eric?"

"Yep."

"Cool. You guys are so cute together. So, what are you up to this weekend?"

"I don't know yet, Steve."

"I have a party to go to. It's my Grandma's eighty-fifth birthday. Can you imagine living that long? I'm happy for her, although she's starting to lose it a little. She's not as sharp as she used to be. I bet we'll all be like that at her age, am I right?"

"Yeah." She mustered a polite chuckle.

To her relief—maybe—Vickie saw Eric walk through the door. He had no expression on his face but he marched with purpose. He took her by the hand without saying a word and led her to the back of the room toward the practice rooms.

Maybe I should have stayed and talked to Steve for a few more minutes. I don't know which is better or worse at this point. But it didn't matter. She was headed to a practice room with Eric, and she had no clue why.

He flipped the light switch on, ushered her in, and shut the door behind her.

It was, in all honesty, barely a room. Approximately the size of two phone booths, there was barely any space in which to stand, and with three chairs somehow squeezed into the tight space, they stood uncomfortably close to one another.

Eric stared into her eyes. She stared back, concerned.

"Is everything okay? What's wrong?" She could hardly get the words out.

He took a deep, nervous breath. "I've wanted to say something to you for the last few days but I haven't had the courage. It's been on my mind, and I can't sit around and let this go any longer. If I don't say it, I'll regret it later. It's now or never."

Oh no, I was right. He's breaking up with me. But why? What did I do? Did I say something? Is there someone else? Will he explain to me why or will he simply do it and leave?

Eric closed his eyes and took another deep breath. "I love you."

Vickie's mouth hung open. "What?"

"I love you. I've been crazy about you ever since I saw you get off the airplane when you first got here. The last few months have been amazing, and I can't get you out of my head. I love you, Vickie."

She froze. *What do I say to that? Do I say it back? I don't even know what that means. Is it polite to say it back? But I don't know if it's right to or not.*

"Th-thank you." Her eyes were wide and she stumbled over her words. "That's really sweet." She pulled him in for an awkward hug and kissed him on the cheek. "I'll…uh, be late for track practice, but I'll see you later, okay?"

His stomach dropped. "Okay." He paused. "Are you all right? Are we okay?"

She smiled at him. "Of course we are." She leaned in and gave him another kiss, this time on the lips. "Thank you for saying that. Really, it was so sweet. You made my day. I'll see you later."

With that, she walked out of the practice room and hustled off to practice, moving quickly so she wouldn't be cornered by Steve Kopitzke again.

Eric, his mind racing with thoughts, slumped into a chair in the practice room. "Yeah. See ya."

CHAPTER EIGHT

Glasses clinked and servers weaved around the tables of Johnny V's on another busy Friday night.

In the corner booth, Vickie, Alexis, Jess, and Jamie sipped their milkshakes and poked at their platters of burgers and fries while they sifted through the gossip and events of the week.

"There is no way Megan spilled that water on you by accident," Jamie insisted. While normally the voice of reason and unlimited benefits-of-the-doubt, Jamie led the charge of accusations this time. "She has targeted you from, like, almost Day One. It doesn't sound like she tripped or anything."

"Nope." Vickie shook her head. "I watched her as she approached. I always do to be on the safe side. She carried an open bottle of water and simply poured it over my desk. I couldn't believe it."

Jess took a bite of her burger. "What did the teacher say? Who do you even have in that study hall?"

"Schumacher."

The other three girls groaned and nodded. His penchant for sleeping during study hall sessions was widely known among the student body.

"Will you do anything about it?" Jamie seemed almost eager at the thought of some kind of retribution for the perpetrator.

This time, however, the vampire wasn't interested. "Honestly? I'm kinda tired of retaliating against her and her friends. It's not like it does any good. I do something to her, it shuts her up for a little while, and then what? A few weeks later, she's back at it. I'd rather ignore it and move on."

The girl's eyes widened. "You'll simply let her get away with it?"

Alexis nodded. "No, Vickie's right. They want you to get back at them. All they do is try to engage you in this stuff. They lose but they keep coming back because they like the attention. Don't give them the drama and maybe they'll get bored with picking on you."

Vickie picked her shake up. "I sure hope so." She brought the straw to her lips. "It's not like I don't want to. I would love to pummel her. She deserves it. But you're right, it's time to move on from it and hopefully, she will too."

The girls continued and made small talk between bites.

"Where's Eric tonight?" Jamie wondered. "He's usually here with us."

"He's out of town this weekend." The vampire shoved a French fry into her mouth. "His cousin is getting married out in LaCrosse, and he's an usher in the wedding."

"You didn't get invited along?"

"No. He said he wanted to, but his parents weren't too thrilled about the idea of having me around for an overnight trip yet. They say we're too young." She cast a skeptical glance at Alexis, who smirked at her. *Apparently, four hundred years old is still too young. I wonder how many hundreds of years I have to be before I'm considered an adult.*

Jess put her shake down and looked at the girls. "Well, I have an announcement to make. Vickie, you won't be the only one with a date for Festival this year." Her companions all raised their eyebrows. "Mark Goodger asked me to go with him."

They shrieked in excitement. Jess was not known for snagging dates—not because she wasn't attractive or friendly but because she displayed zero interest in the dating scene.

Mark Goodger was a tenor in the school choir. He was somewhat nerdy but not bad to look at. Plus, he was very friendly and he was the first guy to show her meaningful attention.

"Jess, that's so great." Jamie gave her a playful punch in the shoulder. "When did this happen?"

"Yesterday." Her face flushed. "He asked me after choir practice. I didn't even know he was interested. He said he usually goes with a few guys from choir but he would gladly tag along with us. I don't know what our plans for Festival are yet, but I'm ready to talk if anyone else is. Vickie, you'll go with Eric, right?"

She nodded as she chewed. Festival was the second big school dance of the year. While Homecoming was held in the fall, Festival was the spring equivalent. It was another opportunity for the students to dress up, vote for a king and queen of the dance, and throw another big pep rally.

"I guess Jamie and Alexis can be each other's dates this year, right?" Jess smiled, knowing that she and Jamie were dates for Homecoming.

Jamie raised a finger. "Actually, I have some news."

The girls put their food down, leaned in, and waited anxiously for her to spill the beans. She hung on for a second longer to maximize the dramatic effect.

Finally, she smiled broadly. "I'm going with Tony Baltutis."

If Jess's announcement came out of left field, Jamie's was from a completely different ballpark. Tony Baltutis had no connection to the group of girls, didn't travel in the same circles, and they hardly knew anything about him.

Alexis was the first to speak. "Why Tony Baltutis? How did you two end up together?"

Her friend waved her hand breezily. "It's not like we're together. We're simply going as friends. Tony is in my chemistry class. He asked me on Wednesday."

"You've sat on this since Wednesday?" Jess was stunned. "I thought I was mean for hiding mine for an entire day, and you've hidden yours for, like, half a week."

"Sorry, girls." Jamie giggled. "I thought it would be fun to announce it all at once like this. I'm excited and he's a nice guy. I think we'll have fun."

Alexis shook her head. "But you're going as friends?"

"Yeah. Why?"

"Whose idea was that?" Alexis sported a half-smile.

"His. He asked me to go with him, and I paused for a second. When I paused, he made sure to explain that we would go only as friends. That made me a little more comfortable with it. I didn't want him to go into the dance thinking that, you know, we'll be together or dating or anything like that. I was more comfortable saying yes then."

Jess winced and shook her head. "Guys don't like to go to dances as friends. He likes you. That's why he asked you."

"Yep." Alexis grabbed a fry and waved it around. "The second you two are on the dance floor, swaying along together to some romantic slow song, the lights dancing all over the gym…he'll try to kiss you."

"Ugh." Jamie twisted her face like a toddler being offered broccoli. "No, he won't. He's a nice guy. He simply wanted to go with someone. It doesn't mean a thing."

Vickie leaned back and enjoyed the conversation. She knew little about how these things worked and she soaked in the exchange.

"She's right." Jess dabbed her mouth with a napkin. "I don't think it will be on the dance floor, though. If it is, it'll be the last dance."

"Why the last dance?" Jamie was incredibly naive about boys in general, so all these accusations made no sense to her.

The other girl laughed. "Think about it. If he goes in for a kiss and you reject him, the rest of the night will be awkward. If he does that during the first slow dance, you have two or three more hours of dancing and hanging out together where you'll be super-awkward around each other. If he does it during the last dance, he can bow out in embarrassment without missing much. It's his safety net. Mark my words. It'll happen during the last dance."

"We should put money on it." Alexis laughed.

"Well, what about you?" Jamie turned to her. "Do you have any prospects?"

She leaned back in the booth. *Literally everyone in the group has dates to this dance. Should I even go? Can I lock in a date? I don't want to be desperate about it.*

"Maybe I won't go."

The protests came quickly from her friends, with Jamie leading the charge. "Come on, you have to go. We always go together."

"Yeah, but not if everyone has dates this year. I don't want to go with everyone and be the seventh wheel or whatever. I'd rather stay home."

"Do you want us to cancel our dates?" Jess asked. "If it'll make you feel bad, there's no point in doing it. Maybe we'll all go as a group like we normally do. The only reason we were cool with Eric and Vickie going was because they are a part of the group anyway."

Vickie nodded. "Yeah, they're right. You have to go." She stopped short of offering to give her date up, for obvious reasons—she had already gone to Homecoming with him, and they had little issues.

There was an awkward pause while everyone avoided eye contact.

"This is stupid." Alexis leaned forward and looked at the others. "You all have dates and you're really excited about it so you're going, okay? And you'll do it without feeling guilty about it. I won't make you feel bad because you have dates and I don't. It's fine, really."

"Are you sure?" Jamie was persistent in making sure everyone was happy. "We don't want this to be weird. Like, I feel sad that we all have dates and you don't."

"Stop it." Her voice grew firmer. "I don't feel sad. It's my fault I don't have a date. You all do and you shouldn't feel guilty about having someone to go with."

Jess frowned. "I'm okay with not feeling bad about having a date, but don't talk like it's your fault or anything like that."

She shrugged. "It is my fault. I haven't put myself out there much. I had a boyfriend but I picked the wrong guy." She glanced at Vickie, who nodded in agreement.

The one who tried to suck the blood out of your neck and literally consume your flesh? Yeah, I'd say that was the wrong guy for you.

"I haven't really flirted with any of the other guys in school. It's my fault. I'm not even saying that like a woe is me thing. It's simply the truth."

Vickie smacked the top of the table with her palm. "Well, you can go with us anyway. If you come alone, it's no big deal. We'll all have fun together, right?" She looked around the table at the other girls, who all nodded agreement. "We don't have to be romantic with our dates the whole night. Let's go together, have fun as a big group, and you won't even notice."

Alexis shook her head. "That's very nice, but no. I won't go if I'm the only one without a date. And none of you will cancel your dates." She spoke quickly to curb any further protests. "It's fine. If I get a date, awesome. But I won't go alone."

Jess and Jamie sighed and struggled to shake off the

guilt they carried from having dates but their friend tried to push forward with the regular conversation.

"Stop being awkward, everyone. I'm genuinely happy for you. Hey, look at me." She leaned over the table to make deliberate eye contact with each girl. "I really, truly, am happy for you. It's awesome that you all have dates. And all good guys, too. Not a weirdo among them. It's so cool, and I know you will all have a great time. I'll work things out on my end. I promise."

They all resumed eating and did their best to shift the conversation away from Festival and talk about other things. But the awkwardness hung in the air for the rest of the evening together.

Vickie was bummed by it. *I was kinda looking forward to hanging out with all the girls without Eric here. I thought it would be a little less awkward than usual. But this is as bad today. Oh, well.*

CHAPTER NINE

The sisters walked into the house. "I don't know what they did to make those shakes, but they were even more amazing than usual." Vickie rubbed her belly. "That was one satisfying meal."

"It usually is." Alexis tossed her house key on the kitchen counter. "Whoever makes those shakes at Johnny V's does fine work."

They walked into the living room and greeted Craig, who swiped through various articles on his tablet while watching TV. "Hey, girls, how was Johnny V's?"

"Delicious as always," Vickie announced. "I'll head to the basement to see if I can chat with Eric."

"Have fun." He looked at his daughter. "And you? Did you have a good time?"

"Yeah, it was fine." She slipped her phone out of her pocket and crawled onto the couch.

Typical teenage girl. Short answers and no information. He returned his attention to his tablet and tapped through a few articles about podcasting income streams and other sponsorship opportunities. "Aunt Renee is in bed," he muttered.

"Good." She honestly wasn't in the mood to deal with her or her dog.

After a few minutes of silence, he looked at his daughter. "Is everything okay?"

She didn't make eye contact with him. "Yeah, it's fine."

"No, it's not." He could read her incredibly well. "I know when something's bothering you, sweetheart. Talk to me. What's on your mind?"

Annoyed, she pushed herself into a seated position and put her phone on the cushion beside her. "Is there anything wrong with me?"

Her father was puzzled by the question. "Like, in general? Or are you looking for something more specific?"

"I mean, like, with boys and stuff. Am I not pretty enough to attract boys? Or not nice enough? What's wrong with me that they don't pay me any attention?"

Craig locked his tablet and placed it on the end table next to him. "Honey, you're the sweetest, most beautiful girl I know. Any boy would be lucky to have a chance to date you."

She rolled her eyes. "You have to say that because you're my dad. Come on, really—what is it about me that turns guys away?"

This is not a conversation you can win, Craig. She'll be hurt no matter how you answer that. Talk your way around it or you'll make things much worse. "Where is this question coming from? Since when are you so concerned about boys? What happened at your dinner tonight?"

Alexis pulled her foot up and rested it on her other

knee. "We got to talking about Festival coming up, and all the girls have dates. Like, I'm the only one in the group who doesn't have a date to the dance."

"Seriously?" He raised his eyebrows. "Even Jess has a date? I didn't think that girl was interested in dating anyone."

"None of us did." She chuckled. "And seriously, I'm happy for them. I don't want them to feel bad about me being alone. But I don't want to go and be the only one without a date, and I don't want to stay at home that night with my dad while everyone else is partying. No offense."

He smirked. "None taken."

"Okay, so what is it then? Why have they all been able to nail down dates in a week while I sit on the outside hoping someone shows me the time of day?"

Craig lowered the footrest on his recliner and let his feet drop to the floor. "Do you want a date because you want a boyfriend, or do you want a date because you're the only one without one?"

She thought for a moment. "Is both an acceptable answer?"

Her father laughed. "I guess so. I simply don't want you to think that you need a boyfriend now because all your friends are dating someone. That's a bad way to go and the entirely wrong motivation. Don't do it to keep up."

After a small frown, she shook her head. "No, that's not why. And it's not like they're boyfriend-girlfriend or anything. Jamie says she's going with this guy as friends."

"Okay, so are there any guys out there you want to hang with? As friends?" He shrugged. "Maybe you could do that."

"No." She hung her head. "The only guy I would do that with is Eric, and well…"

"Right."

"But it's not only about Festival, Dad. It's in general. I want to date. I think there are many cute boys at school. I'm ready to date. I get lonely sometimes, you know?"

He nodded. If there was one concept he was familiar with—especially lately—it was loneliness. "Have you put yourself out there? You say there are many cute guys. Do they know you exist?"

Alexis laughed. "What do you mean by that? Of course they know I exist."

"That's not what I mean." He stood up with a smile and moved to sit next to her on the couch. "They know you're there, but do they know you're interested? If you blend into the background, they may see right past you. And that's not because you're not attractive or desirable, but they may see you as off-limits."

His daughter took a deep sigh. "Why does this have to be so complicated? If there are boys who exist and like me, why wouldn't they say so?"

"Oh, how little you understand about the mind of a teenage boy." He wore a knowing smile. "Can I tell you a story?"

"Do I have a choice?" She already knew the answer. Her father loved to tell stories from back in the day.

"No, but this is a good one, I promise. In high school, I knew this girl named Katie Adam. Now, Katie was an absolute knockout. She was a tall, thin blonde—an athlete. One of the sweetest girls you'd ever meet, right? Katie had a good heart and was loved by everyone, and she was smart too. She was practically flawless, at least from my perspective. And I really had a thing for her. I actually knew her from the beginning of freshman year. We were always friendly to each other."

"Did you two go out?" Alexis hated that she got sucked into the story, but her father had a way of doing that.

Craig shook his head. "Nope. We never did. For four years, I watched her from afar—not like a creep or anything, but as someone who admired her—and she dated other guys. She was popular and only got better looking every year. Despite being so popular, she was never a jerk to anyone. From freshman year to graduation, Katie Adam was a gorgeous girl who you couldn't say a bad word about."

"If you liked her so much, why didn't you ask her out?"

Such a simple question. "Because, Lex, Katie Adam terrified me."

She burst out laughing. "What? How could she scare you? You said she was so nice and sweet and blah blah blah—"

"Like many teenage boys, I was so self-conscious, I never thought any girl would go for me, much less Katie. I spent my entire high school career wishing I could have a date with her—only one date—and I never got it. I couldn't go up to her and ask her out because, in my mind, she was so perfect I couldn't even dare to breathe the same air she breathed. I held her up on this pedestal. There was no way I'd have a chance with her."

Alexis thought she had the story figured out. "Okay, so you're saying there are guys out there who are intimidated by how perfect I am?" She pressed her lips together tightly and visibly showed how doubtful she was of that statement.

But her father shook his head. "I'm not done with the story. On the last day of school our senior year, we passed yearbooks around all day long. You'd catch a friend, hand them your yearbook, and they could sign it during study hall or whatever, and they'd eventually get it back to you. Well, I gave Katie Adam my yearbook to sign, and she gave me hers. This was the last day of our senior year of high school. I thought I had nothing to lose, so I wrote a note in there commenting on how I'd had a crush on her throughout high school. And here's the best part. When I got my yearbook back, she had written the same thing in mine."

"Really?" Now, she was totally hooked. "You two had crushed on each other during high school and never dated?"

"Nope. We never did. We liked each other, but neither of us ever told the other one. I still kick myself thinking about that. I dated some really awful girls in high school, and I could have at least had a date or two with someone I thought was completely unattainable because she liked me too."

"Wow, Dad. Way to miss the boat on that one."

"Right, but here's the point, dear. We both missed out on it because we kept our mouths shut. Neither of us ever really mentioned it to the other person, so we walked through four years of never dating each other, even though we both wanted to. You can't simply blend into the background for four years and think anything will change. You have to take some chances in life, especially in high school."

Alexis sighed and leaned back. Her father put his arm around her and she rested her head on his shoulder. "Why does dating have to be so hard?"

"I wish I knew." That was a thought he still had from time to time. "But you can always take a chance now. You have so much time left. And listen, there's another moral to this story."

"What's that?"

"Even though I screwed up my high school years supremely—and trust me, I would do high school completely differently if I went back now—I still married your mother at the end of it all and she was truly the love of my life. If changing anything about my past would mean I wouldn't end up with your mom, I wouldn't ever take that chance. Never in my life was I happier with a woman than when I was with her. No matter how many mistakes you make, how many opportunities you screw up, and how many bad dates you have, it all works out okay in the end. There's still someone waiting for you, and you'll still be happy."

"And until then?" She looked at him.

"Until then, you keep throwing darts at the wall and see if any of them stick. That's the fun of dating. Don't do what I did—don't put so much pressure on yourself to get it right the first time. Simply take a chance on a cute guy and have some fun. If he rejects you, move on. If he takes you up on it, enjoy it. You can always go back to being scared and alone if it doesn't work out. But you'd be surprised how many great opportunities are under your nose if you're simply willing to see them."

She leaned up and gave her father a kiss on the cheek. "Thanks, Dad."

"You bet."

When she left the living room and headed off to bed, Craig sat in the living room alone, trying to think about the advice he'd given her.

You know, the same thing applies to you. All you have to do is take a chance on someone once in a while. Just because you're not in high school doesn't mean anything's changed. Don't be so self-conscious. You don't have to marry anyone right now but you do need to go have some fun.

After all, that's what Carol would want, right?

CHAPTER TEN

The Choir Hall was baking in the hot morning sun. Because the windows faced the east and choir was always in the morning, the hotter months of the year transformed the area into something of a sauna.

And while some of the students would sweat, no one would sweat as much as Mr Goede, the school principal and choir director.

He was a stout man, barely over five feet tall. His little frame would hop and bounce all around the room while directing the choir, demanding greater and greater performances from them every single day.

All that activity served to work up a mighty sweat, which manifested itself more often than not with several large, noticeable drips on the front of his dress shirt. Because Mr Goede preferred to wear blue dress shirts, the drips were always distracting due to their darkness contrasting with the rest of his clothing.

On that Monday, however, most of the choir were almost sweating bullets, as they called it. Although they had been in the middle of a nasty blizzard barely weeks before, the temperature now rose to more than eighty degrees outside and the choir room heated up rapidly like an oven.

Whenever the heat would strike, the energy in the room could go one of two ways. Sometimes, everyone grew lethargic as the heat lulled them gently and sapped whatever energy everyone came into class with. But at other times, the heat and subsequent exhaustion made everyone loopy and more susceptible to laughing fits.

Class clowns tended to thrive in these situations because the laughs were easy and often. No one pounced on those laughs like Charlie Plamann.

He was a bass in the choir and sang the lowest of the low notes with three other guys. But you wouldn't know it by talking to him. Charlie did not have the stereotypical low bass voice. His speaking voice was much higher, although he was able to reach most of the notes when he sang.

He was an excellent singer miscast as a bass due to the limited number of boys willing to sign up for choir at Clear Lake High School. As was the case with so many other teenage boys, his voice cracked often, especially when he pushed himself to sing lower and lower notes.

Whenever this happened, the corners of his mouth would lower and he wore a horrified look on his face. Then, he would peek out of the corners of his eyes to ensure that no one else heard it. Invariably, someone had heard it and would laugh not only at the squeaking coming from the bass section but also his ridiculous reaction to it.

But Charlie Plamann wasn't a self-conscious guy.

Rather, he enjoyed being the goofball and the butt of every joke. If he got a laugh, he was fine with it.

It was this attitude that made him so popular among the class. Since freshman year, he had been voted class president—not by anything he particularly did but because he was so likable.

During that sweltering day, he already had squeaked a few times and caused eruptions of laughter, even from the normally cantankerous Mr Goede. At one point, the director demanded all the bass singers stand on their chairs while they rehearsed their portion of the song they were singing, a four-part Cappella rendition of "Here Comes The Sun" by The Beatles.

Charlie lived by one rule—enjoy yourself. That never affected his schoolwork and he was an excellent student. Nor did it affect his work ethic and he was a star wrestler. As long as you worked to the best of your ability and had fun doing it, you were okay in his eyes.

And in Alexis Watson's eyes, he was almost perfect.

Unlike other star athletes who were insanely popular, he was a smaller guy. He only stood 5'6", so he never posed an intimidating figure. He was also vigilant about cutting weight for wrestling, so it wasn't uncommon to see him sprint through the halls of the school during the winter while wearing several sweatshirts and a winter hat, working to sweat off as much water weight as he could before weigh-ins.

She sat on the opposite side of the room from Charlie, two rows ahead of him. But because the choir seating was curved around Mr Goede in the front, she could glance at him as much as she wanted to during choir practice without turning her head or making it obvious.

As he and his fellow bass singers stood on their chairs, she all but swooned. *How perfect is that guy, anyway? He's cute, accessible, and silly. I bet you couldn't have a dull day with him around.*

It didn't matter that his face usually bore some kind of blemish from teenage acne to mat burns from wrestling. To her, Charlie was gorgeous and with a million-watt smile on top of it all—the result of wearing braces very early in his life. By their sophomore year, he'd already had his braces removed.

As choir wound down for the day, he seemed to run out of steam and he wasn't the only one. Even Mr Goede, a renowned taskmaster of a choir director, succumbed to the heat. For the last few minutes, everyone was asked to take a breather because there was no point in pushing hard on that day.

Alexis didn't talk to anyone around her and instead, opted to keep an eye on Charlie. She did so furtively and watched him laugh and joke with the other singers. He quickly unclasped the metal watch around one boy's wrist and chuckled when it slipped. When he shared a joke with the boy on the other side of him, they'd laughed hysterically.

He takes his time to enjoy life. I love that so much. He's the exact opposite of Will. When I was with Will, nothing was fun. With Charlie, it seems like everything would be fun. Wouldn't I be happier with someone like that instead? He'd be worth a shot, wouldn't he? Does he even know my name?

The bell rang and everyone filed out of the choir room

to the much more pleasurable air-conditioned atmosphere of the school hallways. Alexis now stood only a few steps away from Charlie when he walked past on his own, his backpack on his shoulders, to his next class.

This is exactly the kind of thing your dad was talking about. Go over there and talk to him. What's the worst that could happen? He says no? You'll never know unless you try.

She slipped through a few clumps of friends until she caught up with him and greeted him with a smile. "Hey, Charlie!"

Surprised, he spun and walked backward to see her tailing him. "Oh…hey. Alexis, right?"

Ha! He does know your name. "Yeah!" She tried to keep her smile under control. *Don't act like a weirdo around him. Relax and be yourself.* "How's it goin'?" *Nice opener. Really original.*

"Good. Boy, it sure was hot in there, wasn't it?" There was that smile again.

"Oh, man, no kidding." *This is the longest conversation you've ever had with him.* "I probably would've fallen asleep if you didn't make me laugh so much."

"Ha-ha, well, I'm glad I could entertain you. I do that to keep myself awake, too. That heat knocks me right out otherwise."

Go for it. This is exactly the kind of situation your dad was talking about. Don't wait until the last day of your senior year. Ask him now. "So, Festival is coming up."

He seemed delighted to talk about it. "Yeah! It should be a good time."

"I hope so." There was an awkward silence. *Don't over-*

think this. You have to follow through. "You are going then, I take it?"

He shrugged. "I don't know. I usually do. A group of guys I hang out with like to go to these things. I haven't really decided. Like, I've already done enough dances with them. I'd like to do something different, you know? Mix it up." He danced a little jig as he said "mix it up" that made Alexis giggle.

Alexis tried to muster up the courage to ask him, but what she didn't realize was Charlie Plamann had thought she was cute for a long time as well. And even though he was playing it cool on the outside, he was covering up for a considerable amount of nervousness on the inside.

Before she could cut through her own nerves and ask him, he jumped ahead. "Hey, if you're not going with anyone to the dance, what if we went together?"

Her heart skipped a beat. "Really?"

"Yeah, why not?" He stuck his hands in his pockets. They were clammy with nervous sweat.

"I'd love to. I actually go with a group of friends and they all have dates this time, so I wasn't sure if I would even go."

"Well, now you won't have to feel left out. Cool. I have to get to lit class, but we'll touch base later. I'll find you on Facebook and we can discuss details." He walked backward again and this time, fired goofy-looking finger guns.

She pointed to him in response. "That sounds great. We'll chat then."

He smiled at her and walked away. Once he faced away from her, he exhaled in a long, slow breath and smiled.

Charlie had asked her out like he'd wanted to and he felt good about it.

What he didn't see was that she stopped walking in the middle of the hallway, frozen in absolute awe that her father's advice had worked so well. *I can't believe it. I'm going to the Festival dance with Charlie Plamann. I have to be dreaming. Someone, pinch me.*

Before she could keep talking, she felt a slap on her back. It was Jess.

"Hey. You'd better get moving or you'll be late."

"Jess...I have a date for the Festival dance." She still stood in the middle of the hall and forced annoyed students to step around her.

Her friend looked excited but confused. She glanced down the hall and back at her. "You were talking to Charlie Plamann. Is that your date?"

Alexis couldn't say a word. She simply folded her hands, held them tightly to her chest, and nodded giddily. Jess squealed and embraced her. They jumped up and down before Alexis pushed her away. "You're right, though, I need to get to class."

"Me too. Oh man, Festival will be a blast this year!"

"I know." She raised her arms in victory and turned to walk down the hall. *It's not like I think my dad doesn't know what he's doing, but holy cow. He couldn't have been more right if he tried. It's like he unlocked this whole new world. And now, I'll go on a date with one of the most popular boys in the entire school.*

And hopefully, he won't try to bite me in the neck while we're out together. She shook her head as she slipped into her Spanish classroom as the bell was about to ring.

She was too excited to pay attention and, in fact, couldn't remember a thing about that class or any of the others she had that morning. All she wanted to do was think about the upcoming dance and how much fun it would be with such a large group.

And now, everyone had dates.

CHAPTER ELEVEN

Alexis couldn't wait to get home that day.

As she climbed out of the car in her driveway, the air seemed to be a little fresher. The sun was a little brighter. And she had a date for the Festival dance.

She felt so cheesy being that excited over a dance. After all, it didn't necessarily mean she had a boyfriend. She merely had someone who would go with her to the dance, that's all. But in high school, a date to a dance was a date, and it at least increased her chances of having a boyfriend again.

With a broad smile on her face, she flung the side door open and marched into the house. Her father stood at the kitchen counter, fixing himself a ham sandwich. He spun awkwardly as the interior door slammed against the wall.

Craig raised his finger quickly to his lips. "Sssssshhh…" He nodded his head toward the middle bedroom door. "Renee is taking a nap. Please don't wake her, I beg you."

"Have you had a rough day, Dad?"

He rolled his eyes and took a deep breath. "Your aunt can

be difficult to handle, especially when she has no place to go." He squeezed his sandwich together and sank his teeth into it. "I tried to get her to go downstairs and go through your mom's stuff a little, but she kept coming back up with some story about an old doll that she found or a photo of the two of them. It's impossible to get any work done while she's here."

She winced at the thought. "I'm sorry to hear that. But hey, I have some good news." She did her best to keep her voice down to a whisper. "Guess who has a date for the Festival dance?"

Her father looked flabbergasted. "That quickly? Weren't we just talking about this?" She danced a little jig in the kitchen to celebrate her good fortune. "How? Who? Sorry...what happened? How did you suddenly wind up with a date?"

Alexis then explained to him her attitude shift and the courage she mustered to speak to Charlie, which eventually led to them agreeing to go to the dance with each other.

As he chewed, he shook his head in disbelief. He always felt his daughter was the perfect girl and that any boy would be happy to go out with her. Now, he heard she had a date with a really popular boy in her class.

In the back of his mind, he wondered whether or not the date was real or if this was some kind of setup designed to humiliate her in the end.

But in that moment, he wouldn't dare say that to her. The look of pure joy in his daughter's eyes was enough to melt his heart. She wore the same enthusiastic expression on her face that her mother had so many times before. He was thrilled to see her so happy and hoped this Charlie guy was sincere.

Craig placed the sandwich on his plate on the counter and took a quick sip of his soda. "You know, when I was your age, my first dates were always dances."

"Oh yeah?" His daughter's excitement levels drained quickly as she sensed another one of Dad's Stories being set up. "So you and Mom went to a dance together?"

"We went to many dances together. But it wasn't only your mother. I took other girls out too."

"Ugh, Dad. Don't do this." Hearing about her father with other girls always made her squirm.

"Relax. What do you think I'm going to tell you? Anyway, dances are the perfect first dates because you can easily go off with your friends if you think the date isn't going too well. But at the same time, it's a low-pressure environment for everyone. You can dance, have fun, and keep it platonic if you need to."

She understood what he was saying but she wasn't thinking at all about keeping the dance platonic with Charlie. She thought he was a babe and fun, and she was very interested in him. Her hope was that the dance would lead to a new relationship being formed—although she wouldn't admit it out loud.

Still, her father had started talking, and he was rolling now.

"I can't tell you how many relationships I had that started with a dance, though." He leaned back and stared off into the distance. "Once, I went to a dance without a date and came out of it with a new girlfriend."

"Geez, Dad, I didn't think you dated that much." She curled her lip with a twinge of disgust.

"Not like that." He waved his hand. "I dated around mostly. I only had a couple of really serious girlfriends. But I had my share of casual girlfriends, too—girls who I would date a few times and then, for one reason or another, the relationship would simply end."

"So what's the secret, then?" Alexis asked with a skeptical smirk. "How would I go into the Festival dance and come out of it with Charlie as my new boyfriend?"

He chuckled at the question. "Sweetheart, that's not really how it works. You can't force that stuff. Go to the dance and be yourself, have fun, and enjoy the music and the company you're with. If it's meant to be, it's meant to be. If you go into that dance with zero expectations, you don't have to put so much pressure on yourself to be what you think the perfect date should be." He stepped forward and kissed her on the side of the head. "I'm happy for you, though. I know it really bothered you to be the only one without a date."

She beamed. "I'm happy for me, too." She strolled through the house and tiptoed past the middle bedroom before she reached the privacy of her room. There, she eased the door shut, then danced wildly around the room with her arms flailing in schoolgirl excitement.

While Craig finished his sandwich, he stared out the window above the sink. *Ah, spring. I love that the sun stays out a little later now than before. If this were January, it'd be pitch black out there already. It's not even setting yet.*

All the talk about high school dates made him think back to his first school dance and Amy Gullickson.

She was a tall blonde freshman girl with braces who smiled warmly every time she saw young Craig in the halls of the school. He had been taken with her quickly, as she was the first girl who ever paid any attention to the awkward, skinny little boy.

When the Homecoming Dance came around, he knew he wanted to go with Amy, but he had no idea whether or not she would say yes. Enlisting the help of Janelle Iwaskiewicz, a mutual friend, he did a little bit of high school recon work to find out more about Amy without ever actually having to approach her.

Within a few days, Janelle reported back that Amy was dying to go to Homecoming with him. So he asked her and they went together as a couple. On the dance floor that night, to the tune of "Breathe" by Faith Hill, he received his first kiss from the girl.

He smiled when he recalled that night and his sweaty palms and his shaky legs. Everything felt clammy and he saw stars in his eyes...until the kiss. Then, it all melted away.

He and Amy didn't last long. A couple of months later, the romance had petered out and he started to move on. But that girl always held a special place in his heart.

As Craig walked back to his bedroom—and also tiptoed carefully past the middle bedroom—he wondered if his daughter would have a similar experience. He didn't know that she already had kissed Will, though, as no one talked about him openly in that house anymore.

I wonder what happened to Amy. She was such a nice girl. I hope she ended up okay. I don't even remember seeing her much after freshman year. Did she stay at my high school or did she transfer out? It's amazing how one person can be your entire world one minute and you completely forget about them the next.

He closed his bedroom door and looked at the wedding picture on the wall of him and Carol again. *And speaking of someone being your entire world one minute and gone the next...*

Even after all these months, he missed the connection he had with Carol. *I don't even know if that's a connection I could make with someone else. But I guess you don't know unless you try, right? At some point, I need to get out there and try.*

Craig thought of the advice he gave his daughter—to take a chance and put herself out there—and he realized that this was advice he needed to follow as well. *If I ever want to get a date again, I have to put myself out there too. It worked so well for her. But she has high school to get dates from. What do I have?*

Feeling like the lamest old man in the world, Craig sat at his desk, flipped open his laptop, and typed *how to date today* in the search box. He chuckled softly in a self-deprecating kind of way.

To his surprise, there were more than a few avenues to find dates. One of them was a website called MatchMe. The description caught his eye:

MatchMe is an online dating and matchmaking tool designed to match you up with your perfect date. Over 7 million members and counting, with a 75% success rate!

He didn't care about the math and simply saw an opportunity to take this the easy way. *I can put myself out there on here. That makes the whole thing so much simpler than whatever else I would have done. Go to bars? Join sports groups? I don't even know.*

Before he knew it, he was building his online dating

profile on MatchMe. He searched for a good, recent photo of himself and found one that Alexis took of him standing on a cliff overlooking the Austrian countryside. With the wind blowing in his hair, he thought it was a good look. *I look like I love to travel, and the blowing hair kinda hides my wrinkles. This will work.*

He tried to sum up his life in as many flattering terms as he could think of—independent businessman, host of a top-rated podcast, father to two beautiful girls. He had originally entered one beautiful girl before realizing he might as well say he had two.

Once it was all done, he published the profile and was automatically taken to a feed of pictures of women on the site who were in his area. Overwhelmed by the sheer number displayed, he decided to close the tab and walk away from his computer.

One big step is more than enough today. I can take a closer look at the whole thing tomorrow, I guess.

CHAPTER TWELVE

After track practice that evening, Vickie joined Krista for the boys' basketball game in the gym. It was the postseason, and the boys' varsity team was trying to get back to the conference championship finals, a game they had lost the previous year.

In all the time she had spent in America so far, she hadn't really watched any basketball. Her mind raced as she tried to pay close attention to the game early on to absorb the rules and try to determine the point of the game. Normally, in this situation, she'd be with Alexis or Craig and she could ask questions.

But her friend didn't know that she was a vampire and she wasn't about to let on that she was. *I'm from Austria and basketball is a worldwide sport. If I admit I've never seen it played, that'll open an entirely new set of questions that I don't want to answer.*

Vickie did her best to cheer when the crowd cheered, although she picked up the basics rather quickly.

However, her worrying about the game was not necessary. Krista was there to cheer on a few of the boys but she was more interested in simply chatting, rather than getting intensely into the game itself.

The two of them talked for most of the duration of the game. The vampire tried to answer in generalities as much as she could, although she had developed a regular story that she told people by that point.

She was far more interested in getting to know Krista. During the game, she was reminded that the girl's parents were both very successful—her father was a police officer, and her mother was a nurse. She had been raised to be very respectful and friendly to other people and also to hold her own thanks to her two brothers.

The more they talked, the more she liked the girl. And it was refreshing to have a friend outside of the house and outside of the group.

After the game was over and the crowd cheered for the Clear Lake High School Vikings on advancing to the conference championships, the two girls were having too much fun to go home immediately.

When they stood in the lobby and debated whether or not to call their parents and get picked up, Krista had an idea. "I'm hungry. Bruegger's is still open. Let's go across the street and buy a couple of bagels. We can call them from there and walk back before they get here. Besides, they don't know the game is over yet."

Vickie loved the idea and was relieved that her companion didn't want to push it too far. After her experience with Tricia, she was on high alert when someone suggested breaking the rules.

The night was cool but comfortable and a perfect

night for a walk. She hadn't worn a jacket, but she zipped her bright pink Clear Lake Cross Country Team hoodie that Craig had purchased for her during the fall season. He wanted to commemorate her making her first sports team, and it was her favorite shirt.

The girls weaved their way through the post-game crowd at the entrance of the building, then freed themselves on the other side and jogged to the intersection.

Once they reached Bruegger's, they both ordered toasted bagels with cream cheese—although Krista chose strawberry cream cheese—and they sat at a small two-person table near the window.

They had both taken the first bites of their bagel when Vickie suddenly felt a chill rush through her body and prickle her skin with goosebumps. "Did you feel that?" she asked Krista, who shook her head slowly.

"No. What?"

"I thought I felt a cold breeze or something."

They both shrugged it off and returned to their food. In mid-chew, Krista pulled her cell phone out of her pocket. "I suppose I should call my parents, hey?"

The vampire dropped her bagel onto the napkin in front of her and looked out the window.

"Is everything okay?" Her friend leaned in and her gaze searched her face.

Vickie pulse quickened. "Uh, yeah. Hang on a second. I need to get some fresh air. Hold up on calling your parents until I get back."

She wandered out the front door and out into the night air, sniffed it deeply, and tried to discern what had triggered her senses. On impulse, she pulled the hood up over her head to cover her hair in even more pink.

It's coming from the right. Go. She glanced around quickly to see if anyone was watching. The coast appeared to be clear, so she surged into a fast burst up a few blocks to the next major intersection. She stood across the street and saw a small chihuahua sauntering through the middle of the intersection.

In the near distance, a black Honda Accord barreled toward the intersection at what she estimated to be forty MPH.

Once she realized why she was there, she bolted toward the dog. The car was inches away from running the poor puppy over, and she careened into the front passenger corner and crushed it, and the force shoved the vehicle fifteen feet to the left.

The airbags deployed inside as it screeched to a stop.

The vampire picked the small dog up and placed him on the curb, then ran to inspect the driver. To her relief, he was the only one in the almost totaled car but he was unconscious from the impact of the airbag, slumped over, and rested his head on the airbag itself.

She was about to pull him out when she heard a voice behind her.

"Holy cow. This is unbelievable. This girl ran into this car and crushed it."

Vickie's stomach sank as she turned to see a young man who held his cell phone and recorded the area on camera. She waved him off but he continued to move forward.

"Look at that. Look at that." He zoomed in on the site of the impact. She glanced over and gritted her teeth.

The brunt of the impact was on the area of the head-light, and it almost looked as though the driver had struck a telephone pole. Of course, there were no poles in the area, so that was impossible. There was absolutely no way that she could explain her way out of it.

The guy with the camera jogged toward her. "Hey! Hey! What happened? How'd you do that?"

She ducked her head before he got close enough to film her face and pulled the edges of the hood down over her face for protection. *The closer he gets, the more you need to go. Start running. Quickly.*

Without tapping into her powers yet, she broke into a sprint in the direction of Bruegger's. The guy followed and continued to film her until she took a left turn down a side street, kicked into high gear, and disappeared into the night—as far as he was concerned, at least.

When he jogged down the side street, still recording, he stopped in his tracks when he saw the empty street in front of him. "What the... Where did she go? Okay, she was here and now she's gone? Something's up."

The vampire weaved through the streets at top speed and tried to be undetectable before she finally stopped around the corner from Bruegger's.

Krista gave her a worried look when she entered. "Are you okay? Where did you go? You simply disappeared."

Vickie pulled her hood down and smiled at her, trying to play it off. "Oh, it's nothing. I needed to make a quick call to Eric before the night got too late. I didn't want to get all romantic around you."

"Whatever." Her friend laughed and rolled her eyes. "I'm

done with my bagel. Now, I have to sit here and watch you eat yours, I guess."

Without a reply, she tucked into her bagel with reckless abandon and ate it in only a few bites. She noticed Krista's surprised expression and tried to act normally. "I was really hungry. This was a good idea."

The two of them stood from the table, and Krista pointed to Vickie's left arm. "What's up with your arm?"

She looked down and saw that the arm was filthy from the impact with the car. Plus, the glass from the headlight appeared to have cut a large hole in the sleeve. "Oh, it's been like this for a while."

"No, it hasn't." The girl frowned and studied the damage. "We've been hanging out all evening and I didn't see that."

"Well, you must have not paid much attention, because it was there." She giggled nervously. "Yeah, I know it looks bad, but I love this sweatshirt so much that I want to wear it anyway. Come on, let's head to the school."

Once they exited the bagel shop, the two girls called their parents, crossed the intersection, and waited out front for them. The crowd had largely dispersed by that point. Before they reached the entrance to the school, Vickie peered down the street and saw the blue and red lights of the police up at the next intersection.

"Whoa, there must be some kind of accident up there!" Krista remarked.

Vickie didn't say anything. She merely hoped to be out of there before anyone recognized her.

At the intersection, the guy with the camera spoke to

the police about it. "I have it all here on my phone. The girl ran up and charged into the car."

A skeptical police officer jotted notes. "So…you're saying she ran into the passenger side? Was she trying to get a hold of the driver?"

"No, no…not into the car. She ran up and crashed into the car. Like, she caused all this damage." He waved his hands around wildly in an effort to get the officer to believe him.

"Do you have any proof of the impact? Did you get video of that portion?"

"No, sir, but I do have video of her running away from the scene and her disappearing into the night. It's true."

Oh, of all the nights to run into the wackjobs. "Sir, I'm not quite sure I understand what you're trying to tell me." He looked at the stoplight of the intersection. "But you see up there? That little piece is a traffic camera. It records everything that happens in this intersection. We'll get our hands on that video feed and we'll be able to see what really happened to this car. I honestly have a hard time believing you."

He brandished his phone with unbridled excitement. "Once you see this and you see the video from that camera, you won't believe your eyes, man. We have to find this girl. She's some kind of Superwoman or something."

CHAPTER THIRTEEN

Craig took a deep breath where he sat on the couch. His sister-in-law rested in his recliner with her feet up.

Earlier in the day, Alexis had pulled him aside and begged him for help. "The girls are coming over to get ready for the dance this afternoon. You have to keep Aunt Renee away from us."

At the time, he had smirked at his daughter. "You know that woman goes where she wants when she wants."

Her eyes stared daggers at him. "Do whatever it takes. Please. This is supposed to be a big day for us, and we won't be able to enjoy it if she's sitting there critiquing our dresses or whatever she'd wind up doing."

"What do you think I can even do?"

"Give her a box of Mom's stuff to go through. Ask her questions about her childhood. Tie her up in the back yard. I don't care. But please let us have this day. It is such a big day for me and the girls and I don't want to ruin it."

He rested his head on the back of the couch and relived

that conversation over and over in his mind. For the umpteenth time, he wondered if there was some way he could get out of his current predicament without angering Alexis.

Maybe I can go to the bathroom or something—she can't get mad at me if I had to go to the bathroom and Renee snuck off then, right? Ah, don't be a jerk. She's right. This is her night. Take the bullet for the team. "You're saying you worked two jobs and was on the honor roll in high school?" He felt dirty trying to sound interested or impressed with what the woman was blabbering on about.

"That's right." She shifted her considerable bulk around in his recliner. He winced at the creaking that issued from the frame of the chair and flashed an angry look at Lucky, who nestled comfortably between her feet. "It wasn't even that hard, either. I knew how to study. I'm not saying I'm a genius, of course, but I managed to learn it fairly early. That's how I paid for college, too. Yep, I socked enough money away so I could attend a good college, graduate in three years, and get on with my life."

How did this woman go to college? And for what? She lives with her mother in a mobile home in the middle of nowhere, Wisconsin. "That must have felt really good to graduate with a degree that was paid for, eh?" *Maybe you can simply watch TV or something instead. Turn up the volume and see if she notices.*

He had almost reached slowly for the remote on the armrest of the couch when he heard a burst of laughter come from down the hall. *That's why you're doing this right now, Craig. You're doing it for them. Let them have this one.*

In his daughter's room, the four girls were helping each

other into their long, flowing gowns. Alexis leaned forward, inches from the mirror hanging on the back of her door, while she applied eyeliner. "I still can't believe we're all here right now. I thought for sure I would spend the night with my dad and my aunt." She couldn't stop smiling.

"We wouldn't have let you." Jamie shook her head while she adjusted the straps on her dress. "Seriously. We would have marched in here and dragged you out if we had to. There is absolutely no way we would go to this dance without you."

She shook her head as she leaned back to check if her eyeliner was straight. *I have the greatest friends. Tonight will be so much fun!*

Soon, the girls were in their gowns. They all had perfect hair, perfect makeup, and they were ready to have the times of their lives at the Festival Dance that night.

Beep-beep.

"Ugh." Alexis sneered. "I don't know why the people in this neighborhood can't use a doorbell. They're always honking to get someone's attention."

Being from the suburbs, Jess and Jamie moved to the bedroom window to see what car had made the noise. They both smiled broadly.

"What is it?" Vickie stepped behind them to see out the window.

"It's a limo." Jamie beamed and headed to the bedroom door. The girls poured out into the hallway and rushed to the living room.

When he saw them, Craig was bowled over. "My goodness, girls. Don't you all clean up nice."

"Not now, Dad." Alexis pushed past him and to the front door and whipped it open as the limo drew slowly into the driveway.

To cheers from the girls, the door opened and four boys decked out in suits and ties emerged carrying small plastic boxes with corsages in them. They all looked very satisfied with themselves—even Eric, who was crippled with nervousness about the evening.

During the whole drive to the house, he was relatively quiet, even while the other boys were talking and passing the time. He was lost in his thoughts. *She never said it back and she hasn't brought it up since. Maybe she doesn't love you. What if she's only waiting until after the dance? She wouldn't do that, would she? This is unbelievable. It'll be the longest night of my life. I should say something. No, I shouldn't. Not tonight. But what if I say something and she breaks up with me? Okay, so maybe I should keep my mouth shut. But if I don't say anything and we stay together, but she doesn't love me, is that any better?*

On and on, these thoughts rambled through his brain. He couldn't shake them despite the fact that Charlie kept the group talking during the drive.

None of the boys really hung out with each other. They were stuck in the classic high school situation of being forced to hang out that night because their dates were friends. As he always did, Charlie tried to make the best of an awkward situation and cracked jokes, asked innumerable questions, and generally tried to keep the guys loose.

The other boys were not as popular as he was, and they weren't sure if he would be a jerk like so many other popular kids in their class. They were all relieved when they realized he was a really nice, friendly guy who wanted everyone to have a good time.

The only one who truly struggled to enjoy himself was Eric. His nerves distracted him at every turn, and a persistent layer of nervous sweat under his suit added to his stress. He hoped fervently that it wouldn't soak through his clothes and show up on camera.

The boys greeted the girls enthusiastically as they walked into the front yard and everyone complimented each other on how they looked. Each couple returned to the house, except Eric and Vickie. They wore polite smiles as they studied one another.

The vampire was equally as nervous as her partner. She still wasn't sure how to handle the situation either. Seeing him standing there in a crisp charcoal suit, navy-blue tie, white shirt, and gelled curly hair melted her. It was a great reminder of the way he made her feel.

He was almost speechless when he saw her with her hair up and wearing a flowing black gown. Her bright red lipstick was the perfect touch, and all he wanted to do was grab her and give her a big kiss—although that would have to wait.

She put in that much effort to get dressed up for you, man. Even if she doesn't love you right at the moment, it has to mean something. Have fun tonight. "You look beautiful."

Vickie blushed so hard her cheeks almost matched her lips. "Thank you. I think you look really handsome."

Erik stepped forward and gave her a quick kiss on the cheek before he took her hand and led her into the house.

In the living room, pictures had already commenced. The two adults plastered themselves on the far side of the room, while the girls lined up in front of the couch. Every typical pre-dance photo was taken—all the girls, all the guys, the couples individually, the couples together, the guys taking the garters off the girls' legs, the girls slipping the garters on the guys' arms, and the wrist corsages placed on the girls' wrists.

Craig tried to take as many pictures as he could and did his best to enjoy the moment while Renee muttered under her breath.

"Those girls are wearing too much makeup. I never wore that much makeup at their age. Goodness."

"How much did that dress cost? She couldn't merely use a dress she already had?"

"Geez, it's not like they're getting married."

Despite those comments, he was filled with pride when he watched his two girls line up with their dates. When Alexis and Charlie stepped forward to have their pictures taken, he lowered the camera slowly and watched the two of them laughing together.

He choked down a lump in his throat. *My baby girl is growing up right before my eyes. With her hair up and that makeup on, she looks exactly like her mother. Oh, Carol, you'd be so proud of her right now. She is such a little woman.*

They snapped one last set of photos with the entire group lined up with their dates, everyone wearing their corsages and garters, before they all finally headed out the door to get into the limo.

Craig and Renee followed them out and stood on the porch, watching as they slid into the limo and screeched at the setup inside.

Alexis was the last one to get in. She lingered at the

front porch for a second, smiling and laughing as everyone got into the car, before she turned to her father. "Can you believe this?"

He cracked a half-smile as he looked at his little girl. "Nope. I really can't." *Why am I having such a hard time with this dance? She's been to dances before. And she had a date last time, too. What bugs me so much about this?*

When he stepped forward, gave her a big hug, and squeezed her tightly like he always did, he realized why this one was so hard. Will made a terrible first impression. He didn't seem to be fun or social because he wasn't. Even though he struggled with watching his girl grow up, Craig knew that Will definitely wouldn't last.

But Charlie was friendly. He gave Craig a firm handshake upon meeting him and looked him in the eye. He openly treated Alexis well and with respect, made her laugh, and was the first boy who seemed to really make her happy.

Combined with the fact that the group was heading to a dance with their own driver rather than him driving them, it was the perfect recipe for an emotional goodbye for him.

"Dad?" Alexis spoke with a muffled voice and tried to push away. "Everyone's waiting for me."

He released her from his arms and held her by the shoulders to look her in the eye. "Be safe tonight, okay? Have fun."

"I will, Dad. Don't worry about me."

"I'll always worry about you, sweetheart."

She smiled. "I know."

Her date poked his head out of the open sunroof of the limo. "Hey, Alexis, are you coming?"

"I'm coming. I'm coming." She laughed when she saw him. "Bye, Dad!" She hurried around the front of the limo to the door.

Charlie smiled at his date's father one more time. "I'll make sure she gets home in one piece, sir."

Craig smiled as he put his hands in his pockets. "I know you will. Have fun."

The party cheered wildly as the limo drove down the street. Renee had already returned to the house. All he could do was stand there alone, watch them drive away, and sigh.

CHAPTER FOURTEEN

Once Craig felt he had his emotions under control, he stepped into the house and braced himself for an evening hanging out with Renee.

To his surprise—and delight—she was not in the living room when he walked in. The TV was off and she was nowhere in sight.

Sweet! Maybe she'll hang out in her room. Or she could be in the basement rooting through the boxes. Either way, did I score myself a little alone time?

Although he was regularly lonely, he appreciated alone time. And now that he'd had it often enough to be used to it, he remembered how much he missed it. The chance to spend a Saturday evening with his feet up in his chair was too good to pass up.

Ironically, the task he really wanted to get to was sifting through his potential dates on MatchMe. Although he had only set up his profile a few days earlier, his email inbox had been flooded with women the algorithms felt would be a good fit for him.

He hoped he could spend his night browsing through profile pictures and get to know these women—as well as he could through profile information, anyway—while he relaxed and tried to distract himself from the emotional stress of watching his baby girl grow up.

Craig put his feet up and pulled up his email on his tablet, settled into a comfortable position, and opened the first email.

Let's see...this girl's name is Sophie. She's forty-two and lives in Muskego, and she's cute. It's hard to tell much from the picture, but that's okay. It's what the date would be for. Hey, she's a fan of classic TV sitcoms. Huh. It's hard to find too many girls like that.

Before he could click the bright blue *CONTACT* button at the bottom of the email, Renee barged into the living room with Lucky bouncing excitedly on his hind legs behind her, panting wildly.

She stood in front of him and held out a huge, heavy white laptop computer and a cell phone. "Here."

He closed his eyes and took a quick breath. *I knew it was too good to be true.* "What's this?"

"They're broken. I need you to fix them."

Reluctantly, he took the devices out of her hands. "Okay...what's wrong with them?"

She waddled over to the other recliner and sat, groaning as she took the weight off her feet. "I don't know. You're supposed to tell me."

"No, I mean, what happens when you use these? What's the issue that tells you something is wrong?"

Renee snatched the remote off the small table between the chairs and turned the TV on. "I can't play my games on

Facebook on my phone. And the computer is really slow, so I don't know if you need to clean something out, or what. Just…whatever. Whatever needs to be done to make them run like new again."

After browsing the guide on the TV, she finally settled on one of the reality TV channels. When it loaded, they were both greeted with the graphic sight of a scalpel cutting into the flesh of someone's knee.

As blood filled the screen, he grimaced. "What the heck is this?"

"Surgery. It's educational."

He looked at her, mouth agape. "You're actually watching a TV show of people having surgeries?"

She leaned back in the recliner, the remote still in hand. "Yeah. It's cool. I think it's fascinating to see inside the human body, don't you?"

Craig focused his eyes on the laptop in front of him. "Not particularly." He stowed his tablet in the side pocket of his chair. *Maybe later, I guess. Sorry, ladies, you'll have to wait.* He flipped the laptop open and noticed immediately that, indeed, the machine was running slowly. A bright red exclamation point flashed in the lower corner.

He clicked on it to bring up the window displaying the available updates for the computer. After several minutes of loading, he was shocked to see the device needed a hundred and forty-two updates.

"Renee? When was the last time you ran an update on this thing?"

"A what? I don't do any of that tech stuff. I only play games on it."

Good grief. You should be thankful this thing is running at all. He began installing the updates and placed the computer on the floor next to his chair.

She peered over and raised her eyebrows. "Are you all done with that already? Well, that was easy. It's a good thing I'm not paying you." She laughed loudly.

"It's not done yet."

"Oh. Will it be soon?"

"Yeah, soon." *At this rate, those updates should be done installing about three or four days after you get home.* He took the phone and quickly found dozens of apps installed that were of no use to her—she apparently simply installed things indiscriminately to her phone. Many of them were harmful.

While he began to uninstall them one by one, Renee folded her hands and placed them behind her head. "What do you usually do on Saturday nights? This?"

I certainly don't do any of this on a normal Saturday night. "No. You know, to be honest, I don't even know what normal is supposed to be. Sometimes I hang out with the girls and at other times, I watch TV on my own. There's also a ton to do. I work on the podcast or whatever."

"Y'ever look at the want ads?"

He laughed at her. "The want ads? How old are you, anyway?"

"What?"

"No one calls them that anymore. No, I don't look at job listings. I am doing well with the podcast, actually."

She snorted. "Yeah, but you can't do that forever. At some point, you'll have to get a job."

Craig shrugged and continued to scrub the device.

"Hey, it is a real job. I am running and managing a business over here."

"Eh, I don't even know what a podcast is. Some Internet thing, I suppose."

He noticed she didn't actually ask what a podcast was. She simply commented that she didn't know and moved on. He glanced at the TV, which now showed open-heart surgery. *I find myself wishing I was the guy on the operating table instead of sitting here with this woman.*

After he'd removed more than a dozen apps from her phone, he reset it and put it on the table. He was about to reach for his tablet and resume his search through his potential dates when Renee spoke again.

"Hey, this is a good time to go through a few boxes. What do you say you go down and grab a couple of boxes of Carol's things and we can sort through them?"

"I think…that sounds like a great idea." He stood and headed down to the basement. Once he reached the bottom of the stairs, he leaned against the wall and sighed heavily. *Take your time down here. The longer you're down here, the less time you have to spend with her.*

He opened the door to the laundry room and yanked on the pull chain to bathe the basement in the warm glow of the bare lightbulb. The storage area next to the laundry room was piled high with boxes of items that had been stuffed there ever since Carol passed away.

This is such a weird situation to be in. You have to get rid of all her stuff so you're not constantly reminded of her, yet you don't want to throw it all away because you want to honor her memory.

A little nostalgic, he peered into one of the boxes and

retrieved a small pair of bronzed shoes attached to a wooden base. On this was a nameplate that read, *ALEXIS WATSON, 2 YEARS OLD.*

He smiled when he looked at the tiny shoes, one of the shoelaces untied exactly like Alexis wore them at that age. *Oh, Carol, I forgot you had Alexis' shoes bronzed. I thought it was dumb so you kept it with your things. I still kinda think it's dumb, but they do look cute.*

The bronzed baby shoes were the perfect example of something he didn't want to keep but also didn't want to throw away. He set them back in the box and pushed it onto the shelf. His gaze darted around the room. *What can I give Renee that will keep her occupied for a while? Something that will take time to sort through but would also be fun for her.*

When his gaze settled on a box marked *PHOTOS*, he knew he had a winner. *Bingo! I'll let her go through these. She can relive endless memories and maybe I can look through those dates while she's occupied.*

Without opening it to look inside to see where the pictures were from, he simply hoisted the heavy box in his arms and lugged it up the stairs. He marched into the living room and dropped it at Renee's feet.

She looked skeptically at it, then at him. "What's in here?"

"Photos." Craig wore a self-satisfied smile. "Lots of 'em. It's perfect. You can spend all night going through these— making sure they're organized properly, eliminating any duplicates. Whatever you want to do. Go for it."

The woman smiled. This was exactly the kind of thing she wanted to do and he smiled, knowing that it would keep her busy for ages.

He retrieved his tablet and sat in his chair while Renee ripped the top of the box open, which had been taped shut. Despite the loud noises, he felt quite peaceful when he opened his email again.

"Ohhhhhh…" She had opened the top packet and tilted her head at one of the first photos in her hands before she flipped it around and held it up for him to see.

Craig leaned over and smiled at the photo. It was a picture of Carol and him at the beach, a trip they had taken by themselves. *Look at how well-rested we are. And how healthy Carol looks. Gosh, I miss that woman.* "Yeah, that was pre-baby, pre-cancer, pre-everything. Our glory days."

"You two were so cute together." She had actually paid him a compliment, although it wasn't the kind he wanted to hear at the time.

When she returned to sifting through the box of photos, he tried to shake it off and go back to tapping his way through an inbox full of perfect matches.

Now, here is Laurie. She's very athletic, which might not be a bad thing. It could motivate me to get off my butt and get in shape—especially if I'm following her around.

"Oh, Craig, you need to see this one." Renee held up another picture. "It's Halloween from the year Alexis was born. Look at this adorable family."

Craig heaved an inward sigh as he leaned over. Baby Alexis was dressed in a black-and-white striped onesie with a matching cap, Carol was in an orange jumpsuit, and he wore a big fake mustache with aviator sunglasses and a police uniform.

"That was a fun night." He let his imagination drift back

to that evening and how many times he and Carol broke into fits of laughter. *No one made me laugh like her.*

He leaned back again and stared at the inbox of ladies. Finally, he shook his head. *Tonight isn't a good night to do this.*

Instead, he tucked his tablet away and slipped down to the floor. He scooted across and stretched to take up another photo—this time, of he and Carol at a mutual friend's wedding.

"You two sure cleaned up nice. You were such a great couple." Renee shook her head.

"Yeah. Yeah, we sure were a great couple, weren't we?" He stared wistfully at the photo for a moment before he set it on the floor and reached into the box for another one.

CHAPTER FIFTEEN

Abby glanced over her shoulder as she tried to casually power-walk through the school halls. *Make sure no one is following you or this whole thing will not work.*

Carefully, she traveled the halls to the back entrance of the school.

Her friend waited on the other side of the door, crouched behind the dumpster with a small mirror in her left hand. She added a little extra purple around her right eye. *That should do the job. It doesn't have to be perfect, only convincing.*

For Megan, this day couldn't come too quickly. She had spent most of the Festival Dance with her girlfriends and glared at her sworn enemy from the other side of the dance floor. While Vickie's group all had dates and were living it up, she was solo—a decision she said was hers but in truth, no one had asked her to go.

The entire evening was spent stoking the flames of her anger and daydreaming about what would happen to Vickie once they pulled this off.

She heard the door open but she didn't look to see who it was. If it was someone other than her cohort, her cover would be blown. To her relief, Abby emerged from the other side of the dumpster. "Are you ready to do this?"

"I've been ready all day." Megan smiled devilishly. "Did anyone follow you?"

The girl looked at the door. "I don't think so. I tried to make sure I was alone so I think we're in the clear."

"Good." She stood quickly. "How do I look?"

Abby stuck her bottom lip out while she surveyed the fake damage. "I think it looks convincing enough."

"You don't think it simply looks like a makeup job I did myself?"

"Well, yeah." She smirked. "But that's because I know it is. As long as they don't look too closely, I think we have a chance."

Megan paced with impatience and a little anxiety. "Good, because if they don't buy it or they work out it's only makeup, we get in big-time trouble."

"Are you getting cold feet?"

"No." She stopped pacing. "But it's a big deal, that's all." She looked at the closed windows of the school. "I had hoped a few windows would be open so someone could hear me scream. Oh, well." She stared at the pavement. "This will look so stupid."

The other girl literally winced in pain when Megan uttered a piercing scream and threw herself onto the ground as if she had actually been struck in the face. She rolled slightly to get her clothes dirty before she slid into a seated position against the dumpster.

Not bad. Abby had to muster enough acting ability to match that intensity, so she ran into the school, yelling for help. "My friend was punched in the face."

The Band Hall was near the back entrance and Mr Mannisto hurried out of the room to see what the commotion was about.

"My friend Megan! She was punched in the face and she's hurt."

His eyes widened and his mouth hung open. "Okay, notify Principal Goede and I'll make sure she's okay."

"She's outside that door, next to the dumpster."

As the teacher jogged to the door, he turned his head. "Who hit her?"

"Vickie Hewitt." Abby raced up the stairs with tears in her eyes but a slight smile on her face. *So far, so good.*

Once she reached the main hall of the school, she knocked on Mr Goede's office door. It opened to reveal a somewhat frazzled and surprised school principal. "My dear, what is it?"

She spoke as frantically as she could and tried to sound as convincing as possible. When the two of them started to move down the hallway, Mr Mannisto appeared at the top of the stairs, clutching Megan's arm.

The girl limped along as if she had been hit by a car. From a distance, Abby was even more impressed. If first impressions were anything, then her friend had scored big time. She looked like she had been brutalized and she acted as hurt as she could.

The principal approached her and put his hand on her shoulder. "Are you okay, Megan?" He looked into her eyes.

She nodded weakly. "I think so."

"Nothing feels broken?"

"No…I'm only in a lot of pain. How do I look?" Another nice touch.

"You look like you've been in quite a scrape. Who did this to you, Megan?"

Here you go, girl. Now's your chance. "It was Vickie Hewitt."

Perhaps the news should have surprised Mr Goede at the time. Vickie had a largely clean record outside of a few fights, she had straight-A's, and she was a star athlete. On paper, Vickie Hewitt had zero reason to fight with Megan Fitz.

But he had been a school principal and administrator for over twenty-five years. He'd seen almost anyone get involved in fights, and even the good students broke rules from time to time.

"Megan, can you talk now, or would you rather go home and rest first? We can have this conversation in the morning."

The girls agreed to come back first thing in the morning, whenever they got to school. He assured them that he would excuse them from their morning classes to have this taken care of. They hurried away and he returned to his office, disappointed that another model student was potentially involved in this kind of nonsense. *I will never understand why people who have so much to hang onto would get involved in these silly fights.*

The next morning, Megan greeted her friend at her locker, a cautious smile on her face. "Well? What do you think?"

Abby's stomach dropped. "It's over. We're screwed."

"Why?"

"Your makeup is completely different than it was yesterday." She leaned in to make sure she wouldn't be overheard. "Goede will remember that."

The pseudo-victim waved it off. "That's not how black eyes work. They don't stay the same until they heal. In the first few days, it changes size and shape like crazy. This is simply a black eye that settled in overnight."

She didn't entirely believe her, but this wasn't her plan anyway. So, rather than protest any further, she went along with it, curious to see how it all would unfold.

As was expected of them, they went directly from their lockers to the principal's office, and he greeted them both warmly.

He eased into the chair behind his desk and pulled himself forward. "Okay, what happened? How did we end up in this situation in the first place? Megan?"

Back in acting mode, she swallowed slowly, tried to summon a lump in her throat, and launched into a monologue she had practiced repeatedly for days.

"Vickie and I don't see eye to eye. We haven't for a while. I don't really know why but we've butted heads ever since she got to Clear Lake. I thought that maybe it had something to do with the typical customs that she had in Austria. Like, there was something lost in translation, you know? But for whatever reason, she thought I was always being rude to her. I know Europeans always think Americans are rude so I assumed that was why. Maybe I was rude from time to time, but I never did it on purpose.

"The first time she got so mad at me, she shoved me in the cafeteria—remember that? There was this weird fire in her eyes like she was determined to hurt me. She did hurt me, but probably not as much as she wanted to. The bigger effect from that day was how much it scared me. I was terrified of her. I still am. I tried my best to stay away from her, but every time I turned around, I had a class with her or was next to her in the hallway. She was always there and always bothered by me simply existing.

"Finally, I was taking some garbage out to the dumpster outside the back door of the school. Abby was with me because she held the door to make sure I didn't get locked out. While we were out there, Vickie showed up and started yelling at me. I didn't even know what it was about. But while I tried to argue in my own defense, she threw a punch at me. I didn't see it coming. She hit me in the eye and knocked me over. While I was down, she kicked me a few times and ran out of the parking lot while I lay there, crying.

"Abby ran to get help while I dragged myself over to the dumpster to at least get myself into a seated position. Vickie was long gone by then."

The speech was perfectly told. She infused enough emotion that it was convincing without being overly dramatic. Mr Goede hung on every word.

Finally, he turned to her friend. "Is this how you remember it happening?"

Abby was almost thrown off by how well Megan acted through her speech. "Um…yes, sir. That's exactly how it happened. Vickie was so full of rage that I felt helpless. It all happened so quickly I couldn't even react until it was too late."

He grasped the microphone on his desk and pressed the button at the bottom. "Vickie Hewitt, please report to the principal's office. Vickie Hewitt, to the principal's office." He released the button and pushed it back on his desk. "I hope it won't be too difficult for you two to be in the same room as her. But I trust you understand that she needs to be a part of this discussion right now."

Both girls nodded. Within a few minutes, a confused Vickie walked into the office. "Yes, sir?" She looked over and saw the two students seated across from the principal, and her stomach sank. *Great, what are they trying to pull now?*

"Holy cow, Megan, what happened to you?"

Megan gritted her teeth and shook her head sadly. "Like you don't know."

"What?"

"Vickie, please have a seat. These girls tell me that you attacked her in the parking lot of the school and punched and kicked her several times. Did you get into a fight with her?"

The vampire was flabbergasted. "Seriously? I've never been in a fight with her before."

Megan very obviously rolled her eyes so Mr Goede could see her frustration. "Of course."

He held his hand out to stop Megan from commenting. "All right. Vickie, we have a witness here who says you were involved in a physical altercation with Megan after school yesterday and that you injured her. Unless you can produce a witness who shows you were somewhere else during that time, I am inclined to believe her."

She scanned her memory and realized that she couldn't prove that she wasn't a part of the fight. For the first time, she had gone for a run by herself because she had to get to work at the seafood place. No one had been with her. "I was alone at that point, sir. I can't prove that I wasn't there but I can assure you I wasn't."

Mr Goede leaned back in his chair and sighed as he stared at her. "Given your history of handling problems in a physical manner, I believe these girls are telling the truth. And I need to emphasize to you that this is not how we handle problems here at Clear Lake High School. And if this is how you intend to solve any issues with your fellow students, you will not last long here."

Vickie braced for the punishment. Would she be suspended from school? There was a big track meet on Friday. Would she miss that, too?

"As for right now, I need to mull over this situation further. Consider yourself on probation. However, there will be a punishment and it will fit the crime. But until I decide what that is, get back to class. You are dismissed."

She opened her mouth to protest but ultimately accepted the decision, glared at the two girls, and left the office.

"Megan, have you gone to the doctor to have your injuries looked at?"

"No, sir. I had my parents take a look, and it appears that I only have some bruising. Nothing too terrible, and it should heal up eventually on its own." She stood from her chair. "I really hope that you can come up with a fair punishment for her. She needs to be taught a lesson."

"Yes, well...that is not your concern. I will take it from here. Both of you can go back to class and try to go about your day. This is my situation to handle now."

CHAPTER SIXTEEN

Vickie stewed in the desk chair in Alexis' room while she twirled a branch of the fiber-optic Christmas tree. For all her powers, she felt paralyzed.

Her sister paced the room in indignation. "They have sunk to a new low. They're setting you up as some kind of attacker so that they can get you in trouble?"

"I guess." She shrugged. "It's working too. I have nothing. I have no way to prove that I didn't do it, and with Abby on her side, she has a witness, I guess. It's two against one."

Alexis sat on the edge of her bed and thought about how angry Megan made Vickie, and how she and her friends would not stop badgering her in their effort to humiliate and discredit her. For a moment, it almost made sense. "You didn't do it, did you?"

She looked up from the Christmas tree, her expression offended. "Seriously?"

"I don't know. Look, I don't have any special powers and they drive me nuts too. I feel like, if I had the ability to beat her up and get away with it, I would try it. And they don't even focus on me like they do on you. If they spent all their time trying to make my life miserable, maybe I'd take a shot."

"Fine. But no, I didn't do it. Why would I beat her up if Abby was standing right there?" She raised her palms in confusion. "Nothing about this makes sense. If Abby's there, I have a witness. Beat her up in plain view and leave? That's the dumbest thing I've ever heard."

Alexis thought back to the times when the vampire had grown impulsive and lost control of her powers. "Yeah, but this kind of thing has happened before. You've acted without thinking and regretted it later." She leaned forward and looked at her straight-on. "Is it possible you lost control for a moment?"

To that accusation, she laughed out loud. "There are two problems with that, Alexis. Number one, I have been impulsive with my powers, yes. But usually, when I act without thinking, it's because someone is in danger. That's when my instincts go haywire. Simply because I see someone I don't like doesn't mean I would lose my temper. Even if she pushed me around, I'm not scared of her physically. Number two—and maybe more importantly—what happens when I lose control of my powers? When I've been careless with my powers around this house, what usually happens next?"

Her sister smirked. She knew where she was going with this point. "You break stuff."

Vickie raised a finger in protest. "No, not simply break stuff. I destroy things. Stuff gets set on fire. It gets bad... really bad. Now let's say I'm impulsive and I've lost all self-control. Now, I attack Megan Fitz as a result. What would happen to her?"

"You'd kill her."

"I'd kill her. If I punched her with the full force of my powers, my fist would probably come out the back of her skull." Alexis grimaced at the thought. "Sorry, I know that was graphic, but I'm trying to make a point here. They claim I punched her in the face and kicked her a few times. There is no possible way she would walk away with a black eye and a few bruises. No chance. This is a setup. She's trying to get me in trouble."

The other girl, exhausted by the near-constant drama that seemed to follow Vickie around, fell back on her bed and stared at the ceiling. "What will you do?"

Instead of answering right away, the vampire turned her focus to the dancing lights of the fiber-optic Christmas tree. She remembered the first time she'd walked into the bedroom and noticed all the bright, beautiful Christmas decorations. The tips of the tree branches glowed from purple to blue to orange to red to yellow to green and back to purple again.

"What can I do? I have to throw myself at the mercy of Mr Goede. I don't really have too many other options."

"So you won't defend yourself?"

"It's my word against theirs. And they have two votes to my one. I don't see any way out of this. I simply have to take whatever the punishment is because there's no way to convince Mr Goede without proof and I don't have any."

Alexis' phone began to ring. She snatched it up to check who it was. "It's Charlie."

Vickie nodded and stood. "No problem, I'm headed to

the basement anyway. Tell him I said hi." Obviously dejected, she walked out of the bedroom.

Alexis picked the call up. "Hey there."

"What's going on?"

"Not much. Vickie's in trouble at school and I was talking to her about it."

"Really? For what? She doesn't seem like the type to get into trouble."

"She's been feuding with Megan Fitz."

He laughed. "Who isn't feuding with Megan Fitz? That girl picks fights with everyone."

The two engaged in the awkward small-talk of a teenage romance to pass the time while enjoying the sound of each other's voices.

"I wish we had more classes together." She groaned slightly at the thought that they never saw each other during the day.

"Yeah, I know. Me too. It's kinda hard to connect and catch up during choir when we're sitting on opposite sides of the room."

They talked about the Festival Dance from the previous weekend and how much fun they had together. She got chills thinking about it. Although she wouldn't say so to Charlie, she was crazy about him and she couldn't believe her good luck that she had been able to go out with him.

And even better, it seemed he was still interested in her, even after the dance was over.

Still, while they talked, she was a little bummed. They hadn't kissed at the dance. She thought that would be the perfect moment to do so, but he never attempted it, although she'd tried to make it obvious that she wanted a kiss. For whatever reason, it didn't happen.

"I was thinking about this weekend." His tone of voice changed slightly and became more serious than she was used to hearing from him. "What are you up to?"

"Oh, uh…" The question caught her completely off-guard but in a good way.

Before she could answer, the door opened and Aunt Renee strolled into the bedroom. She smiled at Alexis and took a seat at the desk.

"Hang on a second, Charlie." She covered the microphone on her phone and looked at her aunt. "Do you need something?"

"I want to talk to you." The woman was very matter of fact.

"Okay, but I'm on the phone right now. Can't it wait?"

She shook her head. "Is it a boy?" Her niece nodded. "You can talk to him at school anytime. You see him every day. You never see me. Besides, you saw the kid a couple of hours ago. There can't be that much to talk about."

Alexis was ready to tackle her aunt in frustration. *I finally have a cute guy who seems like he wants to be my boyfriend and he's about to ask me out on a date. Now, you walk in here and ruin it?* "Charlie, can I call you back later? Sorry, this family thing came up and I can't get out of it."

After ending the call, she dropped the phone on the bed next to her and glared at Renee. The sight of the woman had begun to make her feel sick. Before she could even open her mouth to comment on the situation, Lucky bounded into the room, yipping away, and jumped onto the waterbed with his tail wagging furiously. His warm breath enveloped her hand. Soon, he nudged it with his nose and flipped it over so that he could bury his face in it.

Once he had her petting him, he pushed his way into her lap. *Seriously? This dog is as bad as she is. How did I go from such a great phone call to whatever this is?*

"Tell me about him."

"Who?"

"Your new boyfriend." Renee almost looked irritated by the question. "Come on, I came in here to get the dirt."

"There is no dirt. I'm dating a boy. At least, I think I am. I was fairly sure he was about to ask me out again before you walked in."

"Aw, that's sweet. Where will you go?"

Alexis stared at her in disbelief. "I don't know. You interrupted us."

"Oh. Well, sorry. Hey, you can always talk to him at school tomorrow. Then maybe you can work out some plans."

She closed her eyes and rubbed her temples. "He's a boy from choir." She then explained how they got together and how well things had gone at the dance.

"But you're not, like, boyfriend-girlfriend yet? Why not?" Renee couldn't understand the status of their relationship.

"I don't know yet. We haven't gotten that far in the relationship."

Her aunt scoffed. "Yeah, right. He's a teenage boy. They all only want one thing. If you don't lock him down quickly, he'll keep shopping around until he finds something better."

"You don't know that."

"He's a guy, sweetie. All guys are like that. They're only as faithful as their options. Trust me. Many guys have cheated on me over the years."

Well, golly, Aunt Renee, I wonder why that is? Is it really so strange that someone as unpleasant as you who lives in the middle of nowhere with a dog and her mother would have a hard time keeping a man?

The woman rocked irritatingly in the desk chair. Alexis winced at the sound of the chair creaking under the pressure of her aunt's frame.

"I'll tell you right now, if you went to a dance with him and didn't come out of there knowing where you stood with him, he's leading you along."

She shook her head. "You don't know him, Aunt Renee. And maybe that was true back when you were in high school or whatever, but not now. Charlie and I are fine. We had fun together at the dance."

"Have you kissed him yet?"

There was a pause. "Not yet. But that's not your business."

The woman chuckled. "Listen, sweetie, you went to a school dance with him. You probably danced at least a few slow dances with him with the lights down and the two of you swaying together. Really romantic, right? And you had the cover of darkness on your side. If he didn't make a move then, he's not interested."

Her niece didn't want to hear that—or even think about it. Despite her doubts in her aunt's advice, her expression fell. Renee noticed it immediately.

"But I could be wrong. Maybe he's simply nervous around you. Boys are nervous, too. I'm only saying you should be careful to not get too attached until he lets you know where you stand, that's all. You're a catch, and I want you to be with someone who appreciates you."

Alexis didn't say another word. Rather than sit in the awkward pause, Renee rose to her feet and slapped her leg. "Come on, Lucky. Don't spend too much time thinking about what I said, sweetie. I'm sure that boy is head over heels for you. He's probably only nervous about being with such a cute girl." She turned, walked out of the room, and closed the door behind her.

Alone again, the girl stared at Charlie's name in her contact list. *Is she right? Would Charlie really have kissed me if he was interested in me? He's a popular boy. Maybe he is waiting around for something better to come along.*

Instead of calling or texting him, she threw the phone on her bed, sprawled on her back, and covered her face with her hands.

CHAPTER SEVENTEEN

The following weekend was a whirlwind for Craig.

After stopping and starting numerous times, he was finally able to sift through his MatchMe dates. He was excited to have the opportunity to put himself out there—the same advice he had given his daughter.

However, as he waited outside The Calderone Club—a small Italian restaurant in downtown Milwaukee—he found himself jittery and nervous. *You haven't been on a first date in...what, twenty years? What if they've changed everything about dating and you totally embarrass yourself in front of your date? What if Carol was your only chance at a lifetime of happiness and now that she's gone, you'll simply be some loser?*

That voice in his head was a familiar one, although he hadn't heard it in decades, either. As a teen, he had been terribly self-conscious and his inner dialogue had often sounded like this when he was out on a date.

Once he settled with Carol, that voice went away. But now, it came rushing back to torture him as though it had never left.

Still, he did his best to shake the nerves off when Rebekah walked up to him and greeted him with a beautiful smile. She appeared to be a big Green Bay Packers fan, and she had a daughter of her own. He hoped this would be enough to spur the conversation along so they could both be comfortable through this date.

The Calderone Club was a dimly lit restaurant with only about thirty tables, plus a few outside dining for warmer evenings. Although the days had been warmer as Milwaukee crept through spring, the evenings were still a little too crisp to sit outside.

Craig bounced on his heels while they waited for a table. "Did you have trouble finding parking?"

She smiled and nodded. "Of course. It's downtown Milwaukee on a Friday night."

He laughed awkwardly. "There are some great places to eat a little closer to my house, but I thought downtown was a good meeting place so that you didn't have to do all the driving."

"I appreciate that. So many guys on MatchMe are, like, 'Hey, come out to New Berlin' or whatever. It's nice to see that there are still gentlemen who care about how far their date has to go."

That's a good start. She likes that you have manners. "I find it really depressing that caring about how far you have to drive makes me a gentleman. Men have fallen that far, eh? I'm merely trying to be a reasonably decent human being."

"Well, there aren't that many of you anymore, apparently."

They were led to a small table at the window. It was a great position for a date. They could watch the sunset and enjoy the foot traffic walking past the restaurant, plus the lighting was a little brighter on that side of the room.

"So, you have a daughter?" Craig decided to come out swinging right away after they ordered their food, hoping to establish a little common ground.

"Ugh. I do. And I love her, but she is so much like her father, it is annoying."

Uh oh. "I'm sorry to hear that."

Rebekah pursed her lips. "Dave and I were divorced a couple of years ago. The guy was such a jerk. He never thought of me and never considered my point of view on anything. He's probably still stalking me wherever I go. I wouldn't be surprised if he got a profile on MatchMe simply to see my dating activity."

Maybe you should change the subject. Try to get her to focus on something happy or you'll hear about this all night. "How old is your daughter?"

"Twelve."

"Oh, creeping up on teenage years." He flashed a polite smile.

She, however, wasn't interested in the good. "Heaven help anyone who has to deal with her as a teenager. She told the courts that I was emotionally abusive to her so that she could live with her father. Can you believe that? Me! Okay, I'm no Mother Theresa or anything, but geez. I was the one who carried her around for nine months and made sure she was fed and taken care of her whole life. But because Daddy lets her do whatever she wants, she goes with him?" She shook her head angrily. "It's so stupid. They'll be sorry because I'll move on with my life and be happy, and they'll be the ones struggling to make it without me."

Craig took a deep breath and silently thanked the restaurant for bringing them their food. *This woman is loaded with baggage. Seriously, this is a bad idea.*

For the entirety of their meal, the woman complained loudly about her ex-husband and her daughter and paused only to take bites or belch—an instant turn-off for him.

The remainder of the date was a blur. Between the terrible conversation combined with the appalling table manners, he was relieved when he reached the cool night-time air on the way back to his car. *Swing and a miss. But hey, man, you got out there and went on a date. You can only go up from here.*

On Saturday night, dinner was scheduled with Kimberly, a fitness instructor, at the local Olive Garden. Craig walked up to the restaurant entrance and only saw couples standing around, waiting to be seated. *I must be a few minutes early. Or she's running late. No problem, I'll wait for her.*

A long-haired brunette stood a few feet away from him and smiled warmly at a man who leaned in a little too close to her. She caught his arm and squeezed it as they talked until she spun to see Craig.

"Craig?" She released the man's arm. "Sorry, this is my date," she told him and he walked away sheepishly. "Craig, it's Kimberly." She extended her hand for a handshake.

"Oh." He was thrown off. *I thought she was with that guy.*

They sure seemed friendly. "Nice to meet you. I'm sorry, I thought maybe you were one of the couples waiting for a table."

She laughed and revealed a stunning smile. "No, no. You're my date tonight. Shall we?"

They walked up to the host and he let them know that they had a reservation. Soon, she walked ahead of him and followed the man to their table. Craig couldn't help but notice her when she stepped in front of him.

What a knockout. She looks ten years younger than me. Obviously, that fitness instructor job does wonders for her. I feel like this girl is completely out of my league.

They sat and exchanged pleasantries while the server brought them drinks and a basket of breadsticks.

"I've been single for a long time," she admitted. "For a while, it was by choice, but you know, you reach a point where everyone around you is married and you're alone. That's not to say I want to get married. I only… I want to take relationships more seriously now."

Craig spoke briefly of being a widower, then mentioned his daughter. "She's the world to me, and she's so strong. But she's growing up now. I felt like I couldn't date because I had to raise her, but she's really getting more independent. I think it's time to test the dating waters and see if there's someone out there for me."

Kimberly flashed that brilliant smile again. "That's really sweet. I love that you have a daughter. I find fathers to be so sensitive and caring."

"You're kinda forced to be." He laughed as he sipped his scotch on the rocks. "Not that I was ever a lumberjack or anything, but you can't parent very well if you're not in tune with your emotions. Would you excuse me for a moment?"

He stood to go to the bathroom. While standing in front of the mirror washing his hands, he smiled to his reflection. *This is going fairly well. And she is a bombshell. If first impressions are any indication, this could be the start of something really good.*

When he rounded the corner on his way back to the table and saw Kimberly—who didn't realize he was watching—tug at the front of her dress to make sure that she displayed the right amount of cleavage, it gave him pause. *Well, that's okay. She's probably self-conscious about it. Nothing to see there.*

But as he moved closer, another man walked past the table. She looked up and winked at him. He stopped, leaned over the table, and took her hand. Kimberly held his hand gleefully, stroked it lightly, and smiled at him when he said something to her that Craig couldn't hear.

Maybe she knows him from somewhere. An old friend or a family member. I'll wait for a second longer.

Once the guy left, he returned to the table. He nodded in the direction of the man walking away. "Is that someone you know?"

She looked back. "No. He wanted to say something to me, that's all."

They ate their dinner and every once in a while, he noticed her making eyes at a man seated at another table across from them. He didn't say anything but he noted it in his head.

By the end of the evening, they were ready to part and head to their cars. She pulled him in for a very aggressive open-mouthed kiss. Then, she whispered, "Call me," breathlessly into his ear and walked away.

To his disappointment, this was actually a turn-off. *If I dated her, not only would she be a little too into it, but she apparently can't make it through a dinner without flirting with multiple guys. This might be a bad fit.* He watched her reach her car and admired her figure one more time. *Dang. She seemed like fun. But if I can't trust her, what's the point?*

While most men would have been discouraged by the two failed matchups in a row, Craig was flying high on Sunday. As he slipped his shoes on, he whistled to himself. Alexis walked into the kitchen to see him with his keys.

"Another date, Dad?"

"You got it."

"You know, for someone who has had miserable dates all weekend, you're surprisingly chipper."

He smiled at her. "Sweetheart, if I go into these dates expecting the worst, I'll get it. I'm staying positive. Besides, it's a Sunday afternoon date at the bowling alley. That is as low-pressure as it gets. We can have fun and even if the date doesn't wind up being a good match, at least I got to go bowling."

Jackie was waiting for him when he arrived at the Bowlero bowling alley. She was a little on the plain side but that didn't bother him at all. It was quickly offset by the fact that she seemed to be very nice and outgoing, which made him instantly comfortable.

Once they slipped their rented bowling shoes on and

chose their bowling balls, she lined up to take her first shot.

The ball rolled down the lane and knocked eight of the ten pins down.

"Hey, not a bad start." Craig thought he would be encouraging—after all, this was a fun date idea.

"Ugh." She shook her head without a hint of a smile. "I'll have to pick up the spare."

"You got this." He clapped cheerfully.

She rolled another ball and this time, clipped one of the two remaining pins, leaving one standing. "Dang it!" She ran her fingers through her short auburn hair and exhaled through her teeth.

He smiled politely and took his turn to line up for his shot. When he released the ball, it rolled down the lane and obliterated the pins, leaving him with a strike. "All right!" He cheered for himself and watched the little *X* blinking on the screen. "Strong start."

But Jackie folded her arms and scowled. "Lucky shot."

He was slightly taken aback but tried to brush it off. "Hey, you'll get the next one."

"Don't patronize me," she barked.

Uh oh.

The rest of the date went this way, with the conversation becoming shorter and quieter with each frame. By the time the game was over and he had thoroughly beaten her, she insisted they bowl another game.

"Come on. Don't wimp out. Let's go again."

The last thing you want to do is spend any more time here than you have to. "No, that's okay. I think we should wrap it up."

"Pff. What are you, chicken?"

"Uh…you know, my daughter needs me to give her a ride to a school…function." *Come on, that's the best excuse you can come up with? Think on your feet, man.* "I wasn't expecting to be out long. But it was really nice to meet you. I had fun."

"Yeah, yeah." She didn't even pretend to appear that she had a good time.

Driving home, he felt despondent. *Three strikes. Maybe I'm out of this dating game. If they'll all be like this, I might as well simply stay home.*

CHAPTER EIGHTEEN

That same afternoon, Vickie sat on the unfolded sleeper couch in the basement and tried to remember what it had been like to enjoy the silence when she sat in her room. The basement was notoriously damp and musty, so a dehumidifier rumbled almost twenty-four hours a day.

When Mr Goede contacted Craig about the assault accusations against her, he'd confronted her about it and said he really hoped they weren't true. However, until the situation was resolved, she would be grounded.

In his mind, he worried that the allegations were true. *She has had trouble controlling her anger and her powers in the past. If these girls picked on her too much and aroused her temper, it's possible that she would have done something.*

Truthfully, grounding her wasn't something he was comfortable doing. He had never had to ground Alexis before but he wanted to be a responsible parent while the situation played out.

The vampire understood his position, although she

worried there would be more dire consequences. She simply didn't know how to prove that Megan was lying. On that afternoon, however, it didn't matter.

There's nothing to do down here.

Frustrated, she pushed off the couch and turned on the light above the pool table. She wasn't interested in playing pool, but it brightened the entire basement considerably. Next to an old giant speaker stood a wooden rack loaded with VHS videotapes.

Vickie, not really knowing what they were, picked them up and glanced at them one by one.

The 15th Anniversary of Saturday Night Live? Toy Story? The Pagemaster? What are these things? It looks like they're movies but I don't quite understand what these things are.

She noticed the VHS logo at the bottom of each of the boxes, picked up one at random, and carried it over to the TV. Seated on top of the TV set was a rectangular box, and on the front of it was the same VHS logo.

Hmm. Okay, there's a slot here. And inside the box is this little plastic box. It must go in there somehow.

First, she tried to put the tape in upside down and could only shove it in halfway. When she flipped it, however, she noticed an arrow indicating the direction in which to insert the tape. Following the instructions, she pushed it into what was actually the VCR.

When she turned the TV on, she pressed the play button on the device and picked up the box to look at it. On the front were two young men, both with long hair and one wearing a dark baseball cap. The other one had blonde hair and thick black-framed glasses.

Vickie read the front of the box out loud. *"Wayne's*

World. You'll laugh. You'll cry. You'll hurl." She looked up from the box, confused. "What does hurl mean?"

With nothing better to do, she sat on her bed and watched the movie. The opening scene appeared to be loaded with jokes, while the two young men from the front of the box sat on a couch in a basement—not unlike her at the moment—and screamed at a camera, recording some kind of TV show.

While she didn't understand most of what they were saying, she was curious so she continued to watch.

Alexis walked downstairs and rounded the corner at the bottom of the steps, carrying a basket of dirty clothes. "I'm sorry to intrude. I'm only doing laundry."

The vampire didn't take her eyes off the TV. "No, you're fine."

"What are you watching?" She heard the unmistakable guitar riffs of the *Wayne's World* theme song and nodded. "Oh, you're watching *Wayne's World.* Yeah, that's one of my dad's favorite movies."

Vickie shook her head. "I have no clue what's going on."

Her sister stepped into the living area and dropped the laundry basket to the floor. "Yeah, don't worry. I've been speaking twenty-first century English my whole life, and there are parts of this movie I don't understand either. It's packed with jokes and slang from the early nineties. It's actually before my dad's time, technically, but he had older brothers who showed him the movie when he was a kid."

Despite her confusion, Vickie continued to watch the TV. She could tell that the movie tried to be a comedy but she couldn't quite understand why and she definitely didn't laugh.

"Are you bored?"

"I don't know. There's not much to do down here."

"I'm surprised you're not, like, chatting with Eric or something. That's your usual activity when you don't know what to do."

She looked at her phone beside her and shrugged. "Yeah, I don't know. I feel kinda weird around Eric right now."

Alexis sat on the edge of the bed. "Really? You two seemed fine at the dance."

"Yeah, I know. But that was a special occasion. We've been weird for a couple of weeks."

"Why so weird?"

The vampire hesitated. She knew she could trust the girl with the information, but she also wasn't quite sure if it was anyone else's business. Still, she needed guidance, and Alexis was offering it. "Eric told me he loves me."

Her eyebrows shot up. "Really? Did you say it back to him?"

"No."

She winced. "Uh oh."

"What?"

"You didn't say it back? That's a bad sign. When someone says 'I love you,' they're hoping to hear 'I love you too.' If you didn't say it, I can see why things are awkward between you two."

"Yeah, but I wasn't sure if I should say it or not. Love is a big deal. At least, it was to me when I was growing up."

Alexis squeezed her knee. "Oh, trust me, it's a big deal now, too. And the worst thing you can do is say it if you don't mean it. If you don't know whether or not you love him, you're right to not say it."

Vickie grabbed a strand of her hair and began braiding it—something Alexis had recently taught her. "But isn't that a bad sign? If I don't love him, shouldn't I not be with him?"

"I think you're overthinking this a little." Her sister curled her lip. "You guys have been together for a while now but you're still in high school."

"If I were in my hometown, I'd be married by now." She looked up from her braiding. "When you were fourteen years old, that was when you were set up with your husband. And you were expected to be with him for life."

Alexis laughed. "But you're not in your hometown anymore. You're in the twenty-first century. You're in the United States of America. There are no arranged marriages here. You're free to be with whomever you want. And if you don't love someone, you can still date them. That's cool. Do you think you'll ever love him?"

The vampire returned her attention to her braiding. "I don't know. I think so. He's a wonderful guy. He treats me well and I think he's very handsome. We have so much fun together. I think I could love him but I don't think I do right now."

"Maybe tell him that?" The other girl shrugged. "He might be a little less awkward around you if you say something. What were your exact words when he said, 'I love you?'"

She closed one eye. "I'm reasonably sure I said, 'I'm late for track practice.'"

The answer caused her sister to laugh hysterically for a

few seconds. "Okay, so you didn't really address it at all. No wonder things are so awkward. Sit him down and talk to him about how you feel. You don't have to hurt him but tell him you're not there yet. That's all he needs to know."

Vickie took a deep breath. "But what if that's the wrong thing to do?"

"What do you mean?"

"Like, what if I say that to him and he thinks I won't ever love him? And that we should break up?"

Alexis nodded slowly. She was now beginning to understand what she was so scared of. "You're afraid that he'll leave you because you don't love him yet?" Vickie shrugged in response. "Vickie, Eric isn't that kind of guy. He's really respectful. And if you make it clear that you might love him in the future, I bet he'll be fine with it. He's crazy about you, and he won't simply leave you like that."

She picked the remote up and turned the movie off as it was distracting her. "Do you love Charlie?"

"Whoa, whoa, whoa!" The other girl raised her palms. "Let's slow down a little here. I thought we were talking about you and Eric."

"I know. But you and Charlie are together now. Do you love him?"

Alexis shook her head. "First, I have no idea. That's not how love works. Second, I don't even know if Charlie and I are together. We're only hanging out right now. I thought he and I would get together this weekend, but he bailed. I doubt he's interested in me. He probably found someone better."

The vampire gave her a concerned look. "Where is that coming from? You don't talk like that."

"What? Charlie and I went to the dance together. That's it, honestly. It doesn't mean we're dating."

Vickie folded her arms. "You floated on air all night when you were around him. I saw the way he looked at you."

She rolled her eyes. "That doesn't matter. He didn't try to kiss me and we haven't gone out since."

"So what? Is kissing the only measurement people use to determine a relationship in today's world?" She knew the answer to that one already but she was trying to make a point. "And you haven't gone out since? It's been one week. He could have had other plans or something."

The commonsense approach helped Alexis to not be so anxious about her situation with Charlie. The more Vickie talked, the more she realized she had allowed the bad advice from her Aunt Renee to get into her head and magnify. "So now you're some dating expert?" She liked to tease the girl.

"All I know is Charlie really likes you. I could sense that. It wasn't only about the way he looked at you. A vampire girl can tell these things. Don't assume he doesn't want to be around you because I assure you, he does. Maybe he's self-conscious."

Alexis scoffed at the idea. "Why would a popular, good-looking athlete be self-conscious around me?"

"As I said, a vampire girl knows these things. I can often sense the mindset of the other students in our school, and the vast majority of guys—no matter what year they are—are very worried about how they look and act. And that goes way up when they're around girls. You're a girl, so Charlie is nervous around you. His heart rate goes up. He starts trying a little harder to be himself. Trust me."

Her sister stood and picked up her laundry basket. "Well, I don't know why you're asking me for dating advice because apparently, I know nothing about boys. Why don't you talk to my dad?"

As she walked away, Vickie turned the TV back on. *Wayne's World* might not have made much sense, but it was a welcome distraction from the stress of worrying about her relationship.

CHAPTER NINETEEN

Coach Lueck stood excitedly at the front of the bus, which had pulled into its parking space. He gripped the backs of the two front seats and rocked with suppressed excitement while he made his announcements.

"All right, Varsity Team. Welcome to the first outdoor track meet of the season." The students on the bus cheered with excitement. "We have a good chance to take the gold as a team today, so everyone, really bring it. Let's kick off the outdoor season with a strong showing and let the conference know where we stand. I will hand the race schedule out as you get off the bus. We'll choose a place on the bleachers to unpack, and you can find the locker rooms and get ready. Let's go get 'em today."

The athletes stepped off the bus one by one, anxious to start their competitions. Vickie stuck close to Krista, who had been to many track meets.

But as excited as she was, she was immediately underwhelmed by the location. It appeared to be in the middle of nowhere, not even particularly close to the hosting high school. Empty fields surrounded the facility, which had only two sets of bleachers set up on either side.

"This is…not much." She twirled slowly in a full circle and wondered if she had somehow missed something. "Where are all the facilities? We had more at the parks where we ran cross country meets."

Her friend laughed. "Yeah, some of these meets are really well-stocked with great places, but others are like this. This is Slinger, though. It's about as bad as you'll ever get."

The sun shone overhead and Krista pointed out that this was a very good thing.

"At this time of year, you run the risk of having a rainy meet or even a cloudy one that gets very cold. So much of your time during a track meet is spent sitting around, so whenever you have a sunny day, you take it."

She agreed that the weather cooperated, but she had seen track meets on the TV and they looked nothing like this. "I thought track meets would be filled with people and they'd have all these professional facilities, and equipment everywhere—"

"Oh, it's nothing like it is on TV. At least not at the high school level and definitely not during the first meet of the year." Krista laughed. "Don't worry, they get better, I promise. And if we make it to conference or state, that's when you'll see more money spent on making the athletes feel important. Right now, we're simply paying our dues."

The team wandered over to a set of bleachers that was completely empty and they began to unpack their equipment. Vickie stood at the bottom and looked at the others in her team as they fanned out and dropped their bags on the cold, metal benches.

I know we only used picnic tables at cross country meets half the time, but at least we had a Clear Lake High School banner and tried to set it up like a kind of headquarters for ourselves. This is nothing more than hanging out on the bleachers.

It didn't take long for her to understand why the team set up there. With dozens of different events and competitions during the meet, you were expected to cheer your teammates on while you waited for yours to begin.

Their position therefore made this much more convenient for those on the team. They could still stretch and think about their events, find a snack, or do whatever it was they did to prepare themselves. But at the same time, they had a perfect view of the track and the inside field and could holler and cheer without having to move around.

The team had set up on the left side of the visitors' section. A few other teams had also dropped their bags and settled nearby. Squeezed onto the right side were the fans —parents of the kids in the meet.

Notably absent from this first meet were Craig and Alexis. Vickie had hoped they would come to cheer her on, but they couldn't make it. He had assured her they would come to more meets but not the one way out in Slinger.

Still, she saw a few faces she recognized. Many of the members of the track team, especially the distance runners, were also on the cross country team, and their parents and siblings had made it there. A few of them waved at her as she walked past. *That makes me feel a little better. At least someone will cheer me on. I know why they didn't want to come, but it's my first meet. I had hoped for a little more support.* She shook it off and found a paper cup, filled it with water from the cooler, and sipped it while the first runners of the day lined up at the starting line on the track.

Although the facilities had been underwhelming, she enjoyed watching the events themselves. The boys' team came in second in the hundred-meter dash, while the girls' team came in first place. Vickie cheered loudly for them because she wanted to show encouragement whenever she could.

Krista tapped her on the shoulder. "Start loosening up. We'll go warm up in a second. Our race is coming up soon."

Although warming up was something of a formality to a vampire, she enjoyed pretending to loosen her limbs. With the control she had over her powers, she could easily run all four laps before the other runners even left the starting line—without warming up.

In cross country, there was the added benefit of getting to know the course. Warm-ups were a great time to explore the course, identify problem areas, and generally learn which direction you were supposed to run in.

But to Vickie's surprise, the team moved away from the track to warm up. "Hey, where are we going?"

Her friend looked confused by the question. "To warm up. We can't run this race cold."

She pointed back at the track. "Wouldn't we warm up where we're going to race?"

The girls laughed while Krista put her hand on Vickie's shoulder. "We can't run on the track. There are other races going on right now and we'd interfere with them. In track, the warming up happens away from the track.

We'll go out for a short little run, come back past the bathrooms, and move to the inside field to start lining up."

"Oh."

Another one of the girls needled her a little for the question. "Are you afraid you'll get lost, Vickie? Keep turning left and stay in your lane. It would take real work to get lost on the track."

The girls jogged and walked a quick mile on a short, winding path that cut through an open field. The winds blew the long grass that surrounded them. Krista looked at the track from a distance. "It feels like the wind will be in our faces for the last turn."

"Is that bad?" The vampire hated asking so many questions but she wanted to know what she was getting herself into.

Her friend shrugged. "It's only a mental game. That means when you turn the last corner and are sprinting to the finish line, the wind will be blowing against you. It'll feel a lot worse than it actually is. There's nothing you can do about it except be prepared."

They decided a mile was long enough to warm up and stopped at a small brick building about fifty yards from the track area. The stench of old urine and the musty air of a bathroom facility with no ventilation wafted through their nostrils as they approached it.

"I hate Slinger." Krista shook her head and twisted her face in disgust. "But what can you do?"

Vickie's jaw dropped when they walked into the facility. It was a bathroom and a locker room, technically, with an old wooden bench stretched in front of a bank of lockers on one side, and a line of beat-up bathroom stalls on the opposite wall.

Even with the lights on, the room was so dim, you could hardly see. She walked to the bench and looked more closely at it. Over the years, various kids had drawn and carved their names, filthy sayings, and random doodles all over the surface.

"I wouldn't sit there if I were you." One of the girls stood at a distance with her arms folded. "The rule of thumb here is to touch as little as possible. That's why we all put our uniforms on before we jumped on the bus."

The vampire looked at the few light bulbs that were still working, the fluorescent tubes blinking and flickering. "I can't believe this place is even considered a locker room. This is awful."

"Yeah, well, they don't use it much. It's because they built this facility so far from the high school. Someone has to manage it and no one does. Other kids break the locks and trash the place, so they stopped caring."

Krista laughed as she stumbled out of one of the stalls. "Even a port-a-potty would be better than this place."

Before they knew it, the girls were lined up next to the track, waiting for the four-by-four-hundred relay to begin. Now in their very short shorts and tank-top style uniforms, they were all thankful that the weather was beautiful.

One by one, the girls passed the baton to the next girl in line until Vickie stood at the starting line with her left arm outstretched behind her, waiting for Krista to approach.

They had fought and competed admirably but were in third place by the time her friend reached her. As they had rehearsed numerous times during practice, she began jogging as her teammate approached so she could start building a little momentum—not that she needed it, but they didn't know that.

But to the team's horror, the pass of the baton did not go as planned. Vickie was distracted and a little nervous about doing a good job for the team. She fumbled the hand-off and the baton clinked as it bounced on the track at her feet.

"Shoot!" She bent to pick it up and allowed two more runners to pass her. In the distance, Coach Lueck winced and put his hand on his head.

She immediately felt bad but she knew all she had to do was catch up again. Determined to make up for her clumsiness, she instantly increased speed and gradually inched forward until she moved back into third place.

"Ease up, Vickie. You'll run out of gas," Coach shouted from the sidelines.

The comment reminded her to watch her speed. *This isn't cross country. Everyone is watching you every step of this race. If you can't make it look natural, you can't do it.*

The vampire pulled back and stayed even with the other runner in second place. She had a plan she knew she could pull off without drawing too much attention to herself.

They rounded the last corner and sure enough, the wind pushed all the girls in the face to slow them slightly. *Okay, turn the jets on but not all the way. Time it right.*

She increased her pace, left the second-place runner behind her, and set her sights on the leader. It wouldn't be advisable to rocket past her, but she also wanted to win the race for her team. As deliberately as she could, she mimicked an average sprint and eased it to marginally better than average. She cruised past the leading runner seconds before they reached the finish line.

This was the telling moment. She slowed to a stop and held her breath, hoping she had made it look natural enough and not aroused any suspicion. To her delight, the rest of her team swarmed her and congratulated her on winning the race.

Do a better job catching the baton and you don't have to think so hard about this next time. You got away with it but you won't always be able to.

CHAPTER TWENTY

It was a Saturday afternoon and the sun continued to shine, making the weekend as pleasant as the track meet had been the afternoon before.

Craig pulled on a red flannel shirt and buttoned it up. *It's time to do a little yard work. I've waited all winter for this.*

Fathers like him were generally impatient during the winter months as they enjoyed mowing the lawn, pruning bushes, and getting fresh air. In addition to all those typical father activities, he also enjoyed what others might consider boring or even onerous outdoor tasks because he could pop his headphones in and listen to other podcasts.

It's always good to hear the competition. He retrieved his headphones and slipped them into his pocket. *Plus, it gets me away from Renee for a little while.*

Mowing the lawn was Craig's Time—a chance for him to zone out on his own. Running the lawnmower was almost meditative for him as he could drown out the rest of the world and focus on the task at hand.

Of course, that was if he could get the equipment running.

After tying on his large brown leather work boots, he headed outside and dragged the old lawnmower out of the shed and out into the sunshine on the driveway. He used a gas can stored specifically for this purpose and filled it, then gave the cord a tug.

Nothing happened and he grimaced.

The engine didn't rumble to life. It merely spun for a second and stopped. *Great. Did I do something to break this before I stored it away for the winter?* He couldn't remember any problems with it the previous year.

As he walked back into the garage to grab his toolbox, Vickie stepped out from the side door.

"Hey." He dropped the toolbox beside the mower and knelt to remove the screws from the housing around the engine.

"Hey." She stepped up and folded her arms. "Is there a problem with that?"

He didn't look up. "Yeah. Sometimes, I have a little trouble getting 'er started after a long winter. It's okay. With a little maintenance, she'll be as good as new." He yanked on the plastic housing to expose the engine and set it aside. "Is there something I can do for you?"

"Um, two things, actually." She sat on the driveway and crossed her legs. "First, I need to know that you trust me."

Craig looked up from the engine, a wrench in his hand. "Of course I trust you. What are you talking about?"

"I'm talking about this whole thing with Megan." She leaned back and rested on her palms. "I didn't hit her."

He sighed. "I know you wouldn't consciously do

anything like that. You're a good person." He lowered his voice. "But you're also a vampire and you've had a tendency to lose control of your powers."

Vickie then made the same case she made with Alexis—that Megan Fitz would be dead if she had truly lost control of her temper.

"That is a very good point," he said after she gave the explanation and smiled. "You're not known for being careful with your strength when you lose control of it." Then, his smile dropped. "But that's not an argument I can use with Mr Goede or with the school district. Right now, you have to lay low. I won't ground you to your room anymore, but we still have to tread carefully."

"Thanks. I don't want to lose your trust."

"I know. Likewise. And you haven't. You know, Vickie, this kind of stuff is still new to me too. You've been here for, like, ten months but it's not like there's a blueprint for how to raise a teenage vampire." He cleaned the engine carefully and blew clumps of grass out from inside.

She giggled. "I think you're handling it fine."

"Well, good." He loosened the spark plug and began to remove it with his fingers. "I'd hate to have woken you up from four hundred years of sleep and moved you thousands of miles away from your home simply for you to be unhappy."

Vickie bit her lip. "I'm happy here but there's something that's bothering me. I wanted to talk to you about it."

Craig rubbed the spark plug on his jeans to clean the gunk off it. "Fire away."

"Eric told me he loved me. I don't know if I love him

too. Dating in today's world is very different from how relationships worked when I was growing up."

He replaced the spark plug in the engine and looked up at her. "Did you say it back?" She shook her head. "Okay. It seems like you two are still together, right?"

"We're still together and we do have fun. Festival was a blast. But there's still this awkwardness there. I can't quite explain it, but it's a problem. I think he's expecting me to say it, and…I don't know if I do or not. What should I do?"

"First things first. If you don't mean it, don't say it, okay?" He pulled the housing back onto the lawnmower. "The last thing you want to do is lead him on. But tell me how love worked when you were growing up."

She shrugged. "Love was kinda secondary to everything else. The parents chose the suitor. You didn't marry someone you fell in love with. You had to fall in love with the person you married."

He curled his lip. "Don't be offended by this but that is really backward. I know some cultures still operate that way but I don't think it's any way to deal with love and marriage."

"But what do I do here? I don't know if I love him or not, and I'm certainly not ready to get married."

Craig dropped his wrench. "Hang on—are you concerned that loving him will mean you have to get married? Vickie, that's not at all how it works."

"It's only a thought I've had."

"Love in high school is a little different." He slipped a screw into the lawnmower housing and began to tighten it with a screwdriver. "If you love someone in the moment, you can say it. No one will expect you to get married. But be sure you mean it, that's all."

The vampire didn't really think that response helped. She had hoped for more definitive answers and she still wanted to preserve her relationship with Eric. "If I don't say it, does that mean the relationship is over?"

He smirked. "It depends on the guy. I dated a girl for a while before Alexis' mom came along. And I really, really cared for her. I thought she was The One, you know? She was cute, very nice and friendly, and we got along great. Her name was Kristin."

"It sounds like a good relationship."

"It was." He tightened the last screw on the housing. "We dated for two years."

She raised her eyebrows. "That's a long time to date, isn't it? You two must have really been in love."

He chuckled. "Well, one of us was. See, six months into the relationship, I told her I was falling in love with her. She smiled when I told her, looked at the ceiling, and said she didn't think she was quite at that place yet."

"Uh oh. But you dated for two years."

"Right, we did. And we had a lot of fun. But when she said that to me, I immediately told her not to say it if she didn't mean it. I told her that I didn't say I loved her because I was expecting her to say it and that I said it because I meant it." He stood and laid the lawnmower on its side to expose the blade underneath. "For another year and a half—probably a little more than that, actually—I told her I loved her every time I saw her. I gave her every opportunity to say it whenever she was ready to do so because I thought that was what I needed to do."

"And you thought that would work?"

Craig took hold of the lawnmower blade and wiggled it to make sure it wasn't loose. "I didn't know what I thought. I only wanted to give her the chance every time we were together. I assumed that one of those times, she'd finally say it and everything would be great."

Vickie understood the tone of voice he used to tell the story. "She never said it, did she?"

"Nope. I told her I loved her repeatedly for a year and a half and she never said it to me."

"Did you finally break up with her? You got fed up with it?"

He scraped a few more clumps of grass out from under the mower and tossed them on the driveway. "I never intended to break up with her. I wanted to wait it out and see it through to the end. Until the day we broke up, I was convinced that she would eventually fall in love with me. As it turned out, that didn't happen. One day, we got together for gelato and she told me she couldn't do that to me anymore. She couldn't say I love you, and she couldn't hear me always saying it to her. Apparently, it was torture. I guess she didn't realize how hard it was for the guy saying it, but whatever."

Her stomach sank. *How can you date someone you love for two years and still break up?* "Are you saying we'll break up eventually?"

"Vickie, I don't know the future of your relationship." He stood the lawnmower on its wheels again. "My point is, Eric hasn't broken up with you. He's still there for you even though he knows you're not ready to say it. Don't stress about it so much. If you love him, say it. If you don't yet, give it time. But if you don't see yourself ever loving him, save him the hassle and break it off now."

She climbed to her feet. "Dating in today's world is exhausting."

Craig could relate to that statement. "Hey, tell me about it."

"Arranged marriages sure are easier."

He put his arm around her shoulder. "Maybe, but when you find the right one to stick with, all that other garbage you put up with before winds up being worth it in the end. But stop trying so hard. It'll happen when it's supposed to."

"Thanks."

"Anytime." He pulled on the cord and the mower rumbled to life. With a big smile on his face, he pushed it toward the yard.

Vickie tried shouting over the engine. "Do you want me to do that for you? I can do it faster, you know."

"No chance. This is My Time. Go back in the house." He winked at her as he stepped onto the grass and began to mow.

She smiled and walked through the side door. *I'm not sure if I'm anywhere closer to understanding this, but maybe that's okay right now.*

CHAPTER TWENTY-ONE

"Jim, meet me down at the bar." Pete had an anxious tone in his voice—one that clearly indicated something was up.

"What happened? Do we have something?" He didn't like to wait around for information. He'd rather have the news as soon as it was available.

But the other man had no desire to tell him over the phone. "It's too important, trust me. Come on, I'll buy you a drink."

While he sat at the edge of his hotel bed and slipped his shoes on, he wondered whether this would be good news or bad news. *Is the whole thing shut down? Are we done, and he didn't want to tell me over the phone? I feel like Pete would simply come up to my room if he had that information. Then again, did he bribe me with a drink to soften the blow?*

His mind continued to race but he shook his frustration off as best he could, snatched his key card and his wallet, and left the room.

When he reached the hotel bar, Pete already waited

with a drink in his hand. Next to him was a glass of scotch on the rocks on a napkin in front of another stool. He smiled at his friend when he saw him.

Jim wasn't quite disarmed. *He's smiling, so maybe that means it's good news. Or he's trying to be polite. Geez, you go through this so many times, it consumes you.* Too many times, Jim Trembo had met with someone who broke the news to him that his project had been canceled.

But they had made so much headway and everything was starting to fall into place. They had sent the blood samples to the lab and they had been analyzing the sword they found for several weeks. He was sure those two developments would break the whole mission open.

Yet, as he approached Pete, he reminded himself there was no such thing as a sure bet in his world. He'd spent most of his career being told that he had reached a dead end. He'd grown tired of it.

"Pete."

"Jim. I trust scotch is okay."

"Better than okay. But before I sit, I need you to tell me why we're here."

The other man smiled. "What's the matter, Jim? Can't you appreciate a little dramatic tension? Sit down."

He sat on the stool, still tense. "You reach a point in your career when dramatic tension is overrated. Let's cut to the chase, all right?"

"Okay." Pete took a swig of his drink. "I can only stick around for one, so I can lay out the details. Do you want to start with the blood or the sword?"

Jim's stomach leaped. "The labs came back? On both of

them?" His friend nodded. "Did they coordinate that, or what?"

"Blood or sword?"

"Blood." He held his breath.

"The labs state that the blood is from four different sources."

This was stunning, even though he hadn't really known what to expect. "Holy cow. Something bad went down in that field. Some kind of war? Or a big-time fight, anyway. Were we able to determine what the sources were?"

"That's where it gets a little murkier, but we have a few nailed down." Pete cracked a half-smile. "Three of them are from men of Austrian descent."

"Austria? Well, that makes sense, there are numerous Austrians and Germans in the Milwaukee area. But three different ones, hey? That's something. Human?"

"Yep."

That piece of the news disappointed him. He'd hoped there would be something supernatural about the blood samples. "Dang. I'm happy there was something definitive, but I kinda thought there might be more...suspicious elements, I guess."

The other man raised a finger. "There was one sample that came back a little weird."

"Weird?" He perked up. "Weird is good. What kind of weird? Anything that might shine some light on what we're doing here?"

"Um...I'm not sure." Pete lifted the glass to his lips. "Based on what the guys told me, it's not human but it's not animal, either. No one could quite pinpoint it, but it's definitely blood."

Jim pounded his fist on the top of the bar with so much force that he almost spilled his glass. "That's what I'm talking about, Pete. We have a lead! This could be the supernatural being that tipped off the Superball Project in the first place." He could hardly contain his excitement. "I told you, Pete. I told you this was the one. Hot dog, I'm ready to buy a round of drinks for everyone in the bar."

Several stools down, a young businessman leaned over having obviously heard his reaction.

He waved him off hastily. "I'm only kidding, buddy." He laughed and turned to Pete. "Okay, so that's a huge start. Now, tell me about the sword."

His colleague tilted his head and finished his drink. "That's where things get a little murkier, but in a good way. The sword is dated about four hundred to five hundred years ago. Based on the craftsmanship, their best guess is European."

"Could it be from Austria?" Jim interrupted, so eager to know more news that he couldn't resist.

"It's very possible. Matching the sword with the blood could easily put the sword in Austria a few centuries ago."

He thought of the odd carvings that were etched into the handle of the sword—of a pair of blades crossed over each other and surrounded by a circle. "What about the images on the handle?"

Pete shrugged. "That's part of where the murkiness comes from. They can't place the carvings, at least not from a historical standpoint. There's no common knowledge that references the symbols."

"Is that a dead-end, then?" He hoped it wasn't. They had

gotten this far and he really wanted to push it over the edge.

"Not necessarily." The man dropped a few dollars onto the bar. "It's simply from their independent historical research. We're free to dig further on this and see where it takes us. If we know where to look, we could still crack it."

"So the sword is still on the table."

"The sword is still on the table." He stood. "I'll head to my room."

Jim held his hands out. "Are you kidding? We have to celebrate. This is the farthest any of these investigations have gotten. Pete, I thought you would break the news that the whole project was canceled."

"No, it's still very much alive." His colleague smiled. "We're doing good work here, Jim. They're happy with us…for now. From here, we merely have to find concrete evidence or research or something. It's great stuff, but it's still a little soft." He patted him on the shoulder. "Celebrate for me, Jim. I'll see you tomorrow."

As Pete walked away, Jim pumped his fist in excitement and spun on the barstool until his elbows rested on the top of the bar. *A European sword and Austrian blood. Man, oh man. This is really something. And why is this stuff in the middle of Milwaukee?*

He ordered another scotch and smiled when he realized he had been obsessed with this case for weeks. This was the first big breakthrough since the Superball Project pinpointed Milwaukee.

Remember how excited you were when you got the go-ahead to come here at all? But you'd been there before. You've been all over the world following leads exactly like that one. You thought they were all sure things, but they never were.

Not even that zombie soldier one. It's amazing that the most far-fetched one also felt like the surest one. I thought that guy reanimating bodies would turn war on its head. I should've known better.

But this? It could indeed be too good to be true. But every-thing you've seen so far has been successful on this mission. There is a supernatural...something here in Milwaukee. And whatever it is, it spilled blood in that field.

He took a long, deep swig of the scotch. It scorched his throat and he waved the bartender over. "Buy that guy down there a beer from me. I'm a man of my word."

As his fellow patron smiled and tipped his free beer to him in a toast, Jim felt the sweetness of success wash over him. *After so many dead ends, it almost feels weird to actually be in a position to move this thing further along. I'm not used to success!*

Still, he caught himself before he became too cocky. *There's still a matter of pinpointing what that sword was used for—and why it was here in the first place. There's more to that story. I simply have to find out what it is.*

After paying for his drinks and tipping the bartender, he returned to his room to take a shower. While unwinding for the evening, the memories of failed missions flashed before him. Once he was out of the shower and dressed, he knew what he had to do next.

In every mission, I leave too much up to chance. If I want this to go anywhere, I have to take it there. So they can't discover where the sword is from. Fine. I'll find it out myself. This mission will succeed based on my efforts, not anyone else's.

He pulled his laptop out, sat on his bed, and propped his head up with a pillow.

At first, he stared at the ceiling while he tried to decide where to begin. He searched for connections between Milwaukee and Austria, then tried to find more information on Milwaukee supernatural activity.

Unfortunately, each search brought him to a dead end. Any connections between Milwaukee and the European country boiled down to immigration and demographic makeup. His searches for supernatural activity in Milwaukee turned up nothing but ghost stories and urban legends—hardly anything that one could really dig deep into.

Then, he snapped his fingers. *I've gone about this all wrong. I don't need to establish supernatural activity in Milwaukee. We have a connection to Austria from centuries ago. That's the connection I need to make.*

Soon, Jim searched around for stories and legends of supernatural activity in historical Austria. That's when he discovered stories of the vampire race in Austria and the Sanguinarians in particular.

The more he read, the more excited he became. He knew he was tugging at the right thread now. As he continued down the rabbit hole, he discovered a group of men who claimed to be holy servants tasked with protecting the world from vampiric activity and exterminating any vampires that existed.

They called themselves the Circle.

In the same way that Alexis had been able to search and find current information about the Circle, Jim Trembo found the same sources. It ticked off every box in his mind

—supernatural activity, Austrian origin, and tied to hundreds of years ago.

Then, when he clicked on one website that claimed to be the Circle itself, he saw an image of two swords surrounded by a circle—the same image carved into the side of the sword.

By now, he was almost beside himself and practically salivating at the information. *I can't believe my luck. After all these years, I'm actually staring at true evidence of supernatural activity. Vampires. This sword was used to kill vampires.*

The more he read, the more adrenaline pumped through his system. He learned about the powers of the sword—that it neutralized the powers of the vampire and it was used to destroy them in the great purge centuries ago.

He read as much as he could until his eyes hurt. But when he closed his laptop, he walked over to the window of his hotel room and pulled the curtain back. Jim stared out at the night sky, unsure if he would be able to calm enough to fall asleep.

But how would vampires wind up in Milwaukee, to begin with? Where's the connection between these Austrian vampires and that field?

CHAPTER TWENTY-TWO

Vickie tossed and turned on the sleeper sofa.

Despite all the reassuring discussions she'd had with Alexis and Craig about her situation with Eric, she struggled to wrap her head around the situation.

On the one hand, I care about him, I really do. Maybe I do love him. But how am I supposed to know, anyway? Really? I don't want to hurt him or give him false hope. It's times like these that make me wish I was back in my own time. Things were so much simpler then...

As these thoughts swirled in her head, she finally drifted to sleep.

Her eyes snapped open. The sunshine overhead was blinding. Her feet sank into the soft soil underneath her. She blinked a few times and scanned the area. Small, wispy roots poked out of the ground, and she stumbled when she took a few steps.

Okay, subconscious, where did you take me this time? Why am I here?

On her third step, her ankle rolled, and all her weight

landed on the side of her foot. "Ow!" She fell to her knees as pain seared up her lower leg. For a few seconds, she knelt there, flexed her calf, and tried to send some of her healing power down to her foot.

Once that was done, she stood again. Glancing downward, she realized what she had stepped on that caused the now-temporary injury. "A potato?" She stooped to pick it up and her hand passed through it. *Right, this is only an image. But why did I trip over it, then?*

Before she had time to dwell on that question, she heard a familiar voice shouting in the distance behind her. "Go! Go! Go!"

Vickie spun, excited to hear her brother. He looked unusually tired as if he had been running for days. He raced directly toward her, dragging her sister along by the hand.

"Come on."

The poor girl looked miserable and terrified. "I can't. I'm tired."

"You can't get tired. We have to keep moving."

She looked past them to a group of men who seemed to be pursuing them. The hunters were less than fifty yards away and closed in fast. *Why don't they tap into their super-speed and get out of here? If they're worried that they're in danger—*

Before she could finish that thought, her siblings reached her. She stretched her arms out as if to catch them in a dramatic embrace. As they approached, she closed her eyes, already knowing what would happen. *This is only an image of things that have already happened. They don't know*

I'm here and I can't hug them. Still, she relished the anticipation of it.

The two rushed through her and triggered a chill up her spine. When she opened her eyes, they had already moved beyond her. She turned to where their backs were visible as they rushed onward.

Now, she stood between them and the would-be attackers. Rage burned inside her as she watched these men heartlessly pursue a teenage boy and his young sister. She tensed and shifted her weight to her back foot, so angry at them that she again forgot she wasn't looking at reality.

It didn't matter. All she wanted to do was hurt these monsters. When they approached, she dove toward them. Another chill trailed up her back and she belly-flopped onto the soil, where several potatoes poked through the surface and dug into her ribs.

This time, she didn't stay on the ground. She hauled herself to her feet and raced after the group. All logic had vanished and she simply wanted to save her siblings. She knew exactly what moment this was, and even though she knew it was futile, she would attempt to do whatever she could to try to stop it.

As she got closer, she saw her little sister trip on the soft soil, much like she herself had. This caused her brother, who was holding her hand, to stumble enough that the group caught up to them and surrounded them.

"No!" Vickie shouted and pushed through the crowd to stand beside her siblings, who now knelt on the ground.

One of the men who stood opposite them shouted at the top of his lungs in a very theatrical voice. "It's over, you bloodthirsty monsters. We are here to rid the world of the evil that you are."

Again throwing logic out of her way, Vickie knelt in front of the two young vampires. "Run." Tears welled up in her eyes. "Use your powers and run away. You are stronger than they are. You can stop this. Run!" Her bottom lip quivered.

In the next moment, she heard the unmistakable sound of a sword drawn from its sheath. Vickie closed her eyes and her stomach dropped. *That's why they're not running.*

She stood and faced the mob. The assumed leader of the group clutched a very recognizable sword in his hands. Its ornate wooden handle bore the symbol of two blades surrounded by a circle.

It was the identical sword used in the attack on her in the field behind her house in present-day Wisconsin. She didn't know if her siblings even realized why they couldn't tap into their powers around this group or not, but she knew why. The weapon neutralized their powers.

The man lifted the sword to ear level and glared at the two cowering vampires still kneeling in the dirt. "We have been tasked to exterminate the dangers of the vampire race from the world. Today, we take another step to fulfill this prophecy."

"Please," her brother begged. "Let the girl go. Let her be with her family. Make me your sacrifice and leave the rest of them in peace."

With tears rolling down her cheeks, Vickie looked at her brother. She saw the fear in his eyes and yet, he still did the bravest thing anyone could do. He tried to sacrifice himself to save those he loved.

He trembled with terror but he did it anyway. Watching it broke Vickie's heart.

His words fell on deaf ears. The man took a step forward, swung the sword, and slashed down with it.

She remained between them and saw the blade fall toward her. "No!" she screamed, lunged forward, and clawed at the crowd, irrationally doing whatever she could to break through the image of the event and actually change what happened.

But as the sword fell through her, everything went black and she woke up again, back in twenty-first-century America.

Vickie sat in a cold sweat, her stomach twisted in knots. Her hands were full of feathers. She looked down to discover her pillow ripped to shreds, its feathers strewn about all over the basement carpet.

Her heart raced and she struggled to breathe. Even though she'd never wanted to experience or think about her family's last moments, her subconscious was trying to send her a message. *I've been so worried about these other things—Eric, other high school classmates, making friends—that I've forgotten the truth of this world.*

No one in the world wants vampires. It doesn't matter how good I am. I'm still a vampire, and there are still people who want me dead. And probably always will be.

She stood and paced around the pool table in the darkness of the basement. *The Circle killed your family. They even came to kill you and they almost did it. Why are you so worried about these small things? Your existence is under threat. It wasn't that long ago that the Circle nearly ended you. And remember when you had that feeling that something worse was coming?*

What was that all about? Who else is out there who might threaten you?

Her restless pacing, however, would achieve nothing. *I need to get out into the field and run this energy off.*

The vampire found a pair of sweatpants and slipped them on. But once she reached the top of the basement stairs, she knew she was in trouble.

Even though it was 3:00 am, Aunt Renee shuffled through the kitchen with a bowl of popcorn clutched to her chest. "Hey, Vickie. What are you doing up?"

This threw her for a loop. Whenever she needed to get out of the house, especially in the middle of the night, she could simply walk out because no one else was awake. But with her there now, she suddenly had a problem.

"Shouldn't you be sleeping?" She tried her best to hide her anger.

"Nah." She woman waved her hand. "I've stayed up this late for years. This is my prime time." She grabbed a fistful of popcorn and shoved it into her mouth, dropping several kernels onto the floor. "Why are you up, though? Do you have to work or something?"

"Something." *Why would I have to work at 3:00 am?* "I'm… going outside to get some fresh air."

Renee's polite smile disappeared. "Oh no, you're not."

"Sure. I do it all the time. Don't worry about it."

"In this neighborhood? Sweetie, they have a saying that nothing good ever happens after 1:00 am."

"I only…"

"No! I'd let my brother in law and my niece handle you, but they're both in bed. As the next ranking adult in this house, I'm telling you that you cannot go out there."

Again, she tried to protest, but there was no point. The woman wanted to be in charge, so she assumed the authority. Once she returned to the living room, Vickie stood helplessly and stared at the big, empty field lit up by the moonlight. *My energy will overflow. I don't even know what I can do for myself other than run it off. If I slip out the side door or whatever, she'll catch me and add another layer of unnecessary punishments to my life.*

Vickie returned to the basement and stared at the ceiling until it was time for the household to stir in the early morning. *How do I crack this? Can't I win this one? She'll see me out in the field and I'll be busted.*

Little did she know, the cell phone footage of her colliding with a car to save a small dog, destroying the car and endangering lives, was at that moment being introduced to a local news crew, who dutifully took the bait and analyzed it to determine its authenticity.

Soon, she would wish that the only person to see her expose her powers was this woman, but the world was about to see Vickie Hewitt's vampire powers in action and she wouldn't be able to stop them.

CHAPTER TWENTY-THREE

Craig extended the footrest on his recliner and sighed. It had been a long day.

Hours of mapping out an entire summer's worth of podcast content, weeding the front flower beds, taking down that old tree in the back yard, and mowing the lawn. Craig, you might have overdone it today.

He located the remote and turned the TV on. Within a few minutes, he watched an old episode of *The Office* and chuckled quietly. He stretched a little more and his muscles creaked and strained through the soreness and aches.

I've waited all day for this. He indulged a big yawn and blinked a few times.

To his supreme disappointment, Renee entered the room. *You knew better than to think you'd be in here alone for long. Please, woman, let me have this. Don't change the channel.*

She looked skeptically at the TV, then back at him. "What are you watching?"

"*The Office.* You've never heard of it?"

"I've heard of it." She shrugged. "But I was never a fan.

Come on, the news is on." She snatched the remote and stopped the stream.

"Hey, come on." His patience with his houseguest had begun to wear thin. "I was watching that."

Ignoring him, she sat and stared at the TV while she navigated to the local news. "We gotta know what's going on in the world. Who better to hear it from than your local news anchor?"

Craig thought about arguing with her but talked himself out of it. *She'll be gone soon. Don't bother driving the drama up now because it won't change her or make her leave any sooner. Suck it up and deal with it.*

Once satisfied with the right news channel, Renee leaned back in the chair, which creaked under her weight. In his mind, he wondered how much damage she was doing to the recliner.

Regardless, he accepted his fate and watched the news. His body was too tired to get a book anyway.

"Good evening, and welcome to the Channel Six News at 6:30. I'm Ted Percival. Our top story tonight. A mysterious video has gone viral online, claiming to be recorded in Milwaukee. Some say it's a clever hoax, while others insist it is real. Fred Francis has more..."

The video replayed with no sound and a bold title scrolling across the bottom of the screen labeled, *VIRAL VIDEO: REAL OR HOAX?* It depicted a young girl in a pink hooded sweatshirt lowering her shoulder and crashing into the front end of a car to prevent it from running over a small dog.

This video was an overhead shot from the traffic camera, showing the full extent of the incident. Then, it switched to a video recorded on a phone of the aftermath, including the supposed disappearance of the girl down a side street.

As the news switched between the two clips, a male voice narrated:

"Earlier this month, an accident was reported on the lower west side of Milwaukee. It was a one-car crash, although it was not apparent what the car struck. Initially, the police believed there to be a second vehicle involved, given the extent of the damage done to the vehicle. But once they saw the traffic camera feed, they had a different story entirely. The video appears to show someone running into the street and deliberately impacting into the car, knocking it away from the dog it was about to run over.

"The severity of the collision left the car with a badly damaged front bumper and a shattered headlight, and it even deployed the airbag. The driver claims he did not see anything before the impact.

"I asked Milwaukee Sheriff Clark Duncan why it had taken so long to release the footage.

"'Frankly, we weren't sure what we were looking at. Some of us even believed that the traffic camera itself was tampered with. But for whatever reason, this video appears to be legitimate and we wanted answers. We've studied this over and over again, and we haven't been able to connect any dots. That's why we finally went public with the video.'"

Craig's stomach dropped. *I know who's in that video.* He shot a glance at Renee, whose eyebrows were raised.

"That is crazy. But there's no way that's real. It has to be a fake. People fake videos all the time. I bet some hacker tapped into the traffic camera and uploaded this or something. There is no chance a human being did that."

Nope, no human being did that, you're right there. But a vampire maybe. Craig rested his cheek on his fist for a moment while he watched the rest of the segment.

"The man who recorded the aftermath on his cell phone says he thought he was seeing things, but after rewatching the video several times, he's convinced he saw something supernatural.

"'There's no way you can convince me a human did that. It was a teenage girl, but she hit that car like a Mack truck. I pulled my phone out to record it because I was in shock. All I knew was I needed to get it on record. There were no other witnesses paying attention at the time, I guess. But I saw what I saw, and when I chased after her, she disappeared right before my eyes.'

"The Milwaukee Police Department urges anyone who has information on the young woman in the video to call the phone number on your screen, but be advised that callers will be taken seriously, and we are asked to not clog the phone lines up with prank callers or deliberately misleading information."

Renee looked at Craig. "You see? This is the kind of stuff you should watch. Who needs to see another episode of *The Office* for the forty-sixth time when you have a monster running loose in the streets of the city. That's your real drama right there." She rocked enthusiastically in the chair. "Man, I love watching the news in big cities. Stuff like this never happens in Tomahawk."

Craig hardly heard a word she spoke, however. He was

too busy thinking about Vickie. He stood from his chair and walked out of the room and into the basement.

Once he reached the bottom of the stairs, he saw Vickie seated and doing homework on her laptop. "I need to talk to you."

She turned her head but kept her gaze on the screen. "Right now? Can it wait? I'm in the middle of something."

He stepped forward. "Did you destroy a car on the street earlier this month?"

Now, he had her full attention. She dragged her gaze away from her laptop and looked at him. "Um…"

"Are you kidding me?" He sat on the edge of her bed. "I have so many questions to ask right now, and none of them are good."

"Can I say something?"

"Fine."

With a sigh, she closed her laptop and set it beside her hip. "I was out after a meet. Krista and I got bagels, and my senses went off. I had to react."

Craig shook his head. "At what point can you simply ignore your senses? You've had control over this for some time now. Can't you move past them and stay with whatever it is you're doing in that moment?"

Vickie hesitated before she spoke again. "I'm not…my senses are tripped when innocent beings are in danger. Sometimes, that being is me. Sometimes, it's you or Alexis. Or it's a child playing on a sidewalk. In this case, it was a dog. I didn't know it was a dog. I only knew it was innocent. If I am within a reasonable range to do something about it and fix it, I am pulled from wherever I am to try to save it."

How the heck am I supposed to argue with that? "Vickie, I'm very glad your senses allow you the ability to do some good in the world. I know you can save lives with your powers, and that's important to remember. But you can't be this careless with it. Now, you're on the news, and the police department wants to have you arrested for causing this crash."

This confused her. "But my hood was up. Everything was tucked away. I don't think anyone could recognize me only from my clothes."

Just then, the two of them heard footsteps descend the stairs. They stopped talking for a moment, hoping that it wasn't Aunt Renee, but it was Alexis.

She waved the phone in her hand. "Have you guys seen this video? Vickie, you totally smashed a car. It's being shared hundreds of times on Facebook now."

Craig turned back to the vampire with an I told you so look on his face. Her expression fell.

"That's what we were talking about, honey." He tilted his head to stretch his neck muscles. "Vickie saved a dog and now she's on the news and spread all over social media. This is bad, Vickie. Really bad."

Of course, she felt guilty. *I simply tried to do a good thing for a puppy. Now, I'm made out to be some kind of enemy? Seriously?* "What am I supposed to do? Fight every instinct inside me? Bury the vampire blood in my veins? Stop being who I am?"

Alexis leaned against the wall. "I don't think you have to go that far. But think about it like this. If you keep doing stuff like this, you run the risk of getting caught. And then what? This is really close."

Vickie thought back to her feelings that something worse than the Circle was hunting her again. *Will this exposure lead them to me now?* "I don't want to get caught."

"Of course you don't." He patted her on the shin. "And we'll try to keep finding ways for you to work out your energy if you need it. But you can't walk around destroying things in full view of the public and not expect to get caught at some point."

"Dad, do you think she'll be caught this time?"

Craig looked out the window. "I'm not sure about anything. I hope that no one can recognize her with her hood pulled over her head like it is on the video. I think that's our only hope—that her face was concealed enough to keep people from catching on."

Vickie looked dejected. *All I want to do is help, and I only seem to screw it up.*

"Listen, I'm happy you're trying to use your powers for good." He leaned forward so she would look into his eyes and know he was serious. "I love it, actually. You have a great heart. But you can't keep doing this. You have to stop or find a way to avoid putting yourself into those situations."

CHAPTER TWENTY-FOUR

Alexis strolled through the halls on a rather busy Monday morning at school.

For whatever reason, the energy levels among the student body were at an all-time high. The jocks horsed around in one hall and the nerds passionately argued the merits of Disney owning the *Star Wars* franchise in another. Couples broke up in huge public arguments.

It was enough to make her want to claim illness and hang out at the nurse's office for a couple of hours.

Instead, she sought refuge in one of the few quiet places in the entire school—the Art Hall.

This area was unique. Students didn't generally go down there by accident or in passing because it was only one-way. It was the only hall blocked by a set of double doors, and on the other side of those were several classrooms devoted to artistic pursuits—ceramics, painting, sketching, and so on.

At the end of the hall was nothing at all—only an office

for the art teachers, and that was it. The classes were usually taught later in the day, so while the hall was open like any other in the school, it was almost always empty.

Because it was so secluded, however, it was also the target for more than a few not so artistic activities. Depending on the time of day, it hosted students making out or fooling around. One pair of students were allegedly caught doing something in there that no one spoke about in any detail but they were both expelled for it.

For Alexis, the Art Hall was a fortress. She enjoyed wandering through and staring at the completed pieces hanging on the walls. There, she could surround herself with beauty and silence and take a break from the rigors of high school.

The long space was shaped like an L, with a sharp left turn at one end leading to a drawing classroom. What she didn't know was that on the other side of that L, Megan and Abby were in the middle of a private conversation.

She stepped into the hall, closed the double doors behind her, and immediately enveloped herself with silence. A small smile settled onto her face when she saw the hallway stretch out in front of her with updated works of art. The most recent project for the painting class was to create a vase of flowers, and the colors were vibrant and stunning. She moved forward a little more, removed herself from the rest of the world, and simply enjoyed the talents of her fellow students.

But when she heard low voices coming from around the corner, she paused.

"She's not suspended yet? Are you kidding?"

"I'm trying to make my case, but I don't know why they're dragging their feet."

Like any young person, Alexis was intrigued by what appeared to be dirt on a fellow student. She ducked into the doorway of the ceramics classroom to listen in. When she peered around the corner and saw that it was Megan and Abby, she grew nervous. *Great, I bet I know what this is about.* She slipped her phone quickly out of her pocket and put it on silent so that the noise of the camera's shutter button wouldn't click. When she'd double-checked that, she switched it to Video Mode and started to record, hoping that the low voices would be picked up by the microphone.

Abby sounded desperate. "I really put my reputation on the line here. What if I get caught lying?"

Megan tried to reassure her. "Relax. You won't get caught lying. I've done a really convincing job on my makeup. To anyone who asks, this is the real deal. I even fooled Mr Goede."

"But if they believe you, why is she still here? I saw this morning's announcements and she was named as part of the winning track team from last weekend's meet. Like, if she beat you up, why is she still being treated like a hero?"

The other girl rolled her eyes. "This is a long game. If we want her to look bad and if we want her to be punished and finally get some retribution, we have to wait it out. She'll be suspended or something and we can laugh at her for it. You simply have to hang in there."

Abby sighed. "I have another meeting with Mr Goede today. He wants me to go over the details of the attack with him so he can be sure our stories match."

"You'd better be convincing." Megan poked her threateningly in the chest. "Maybe we can have her suspended by the end of this week yet."

Her friend slapped her hand away. "Back off. Making this up wasn't my idea. If this doesn't work, it's your fault, not mine."

Alexis pumped her fist as she deactivated her phone's camera and stuck it back into her pocket. *They're dead. I have their confession on camera.*

However, even though she was excited, she also burned with rage. *I can't believe those two would stoop this low to get at Vickie. She has a hard-enough time without people making up wild accusations against her. This could ruin the little reputation she has.*

"What's great about how this is going to work is that it'll make her look really bad on top of it." Megan sounded almost maniacal in her obsession over this plan. "First, we have to convince Mr Goede and maybe a few teachers. Once it's known and confirmed as fact, we spread the word around school. Maybe we can embarrass her enough to get her to leave."

"Can you imagine?" Abby sighed. "Finally getting her out of here and returning things to the way they used to be. That would be so great."

Alexis strode out of the doorway and turned the corner to face them both. Her sudden appearance startled them.

"What do you want?" Megan gave her a disgusted face.

"To give you a black eye." She sneered with real disgust.

The girl scoffed and pointed to the makeup around her eye. "Yeah, I already have one, babe."

She dropped her backpack. "No, I mean a real one."

The two girls looked worriedly at one another. Those words meant that the newcomer knew what they were up to. Before they could react, she charged at them both and tackled Abby, who fell heavily.

Megan jumped on top of her and threw a few punches at her face before Alexis shoved away from Abby and threw herself back to thrust the other girl off her. She grabbed her by the hair while she screamed, "I've had enough of you spending all your time trying to make Vickie miserable."

The girl clamped her eyes shut when Alexis drew her hand back, ready to give her the well-deserved black eye.

But as luck would have it, Mr Bintz, the drawing teacher, had work he needed to get to early. As he walked around the corner of the Art Hall and saw three girls engaged in a fistfight, his eyes widened, and he began to shout. "Stop it! All of you!"

Minutes later, the three girls sat at Mr Goede's desk in his office. Alexis' cheek burned where the bruises on her cheekbone began to rise. Megan had a fierce headache from her hair being pulled, and Abby's back and head both ached from the impact of hitting the floor.

"This is not conduct befitting members of Clear Lake High School." Mr Goede seethed with rage. "Now, we already have one act of violence that I am in the middle of dealing with. Does there need to be a second one?"

Alexis raised her hand slowly. "Mr Goede? I have a video you need to watch. It's about that first act of violence." She directed a sarcastic look at the two girls as she said it.

The principal watched the video and scowled at the

inadvertent confession. He looked up from the phone at the two culprits. "You have wasted my time, others' time, and the school's valuable resources to investigate your false claim. There will be consequences for this, starting with a month's detention. Go home. You are both are suspended for the next two days."

The girls tried to protest but he wouldn't hear of it and instead, pointed to the door.

Once they were gone, he turned his attention to Alexis. "Young lady, I appreciate the information you have provided and that you were looking out for your cousin. However, violence is not an acceptable solution to this problem."

"Yes, sir."

"This is not how adults handle these situations. Had you recorded the video and simply came to me, you would be in the clear. But because you decided to react physically, I have no choice but to punish you as well. You will have one week of detention and you will also be suspended for the next two days."

She walked out of Mr Goede's office and retrieved a few things from her locker before she stepped out the front entrance to wait for her dad. Briefly, she wondered if the other two girls would be outside waiting for their rides— and if she would react violently to them again.

But they were, thankfully, nowhere to be seen and Alexis sat on the metal bench to wait for her father.

The ride home was silent for the first ten minutes of the twenty-minute drive. Craig stewed in his anger at his daughter, flabbergasted that she would be driven to fight anyone at school. *That's not my daughter. She wouldn't do something like that. Where do I even begin? I don't know what to say to her.*

Finally, he broke the silence. "In what world—in what universe—have I ever condoned physical violence against other students? I don't even know who you are right now. My little girl would never do something like this."

"Dad—"

He wasn't done yet and gave her protest no time to gain momentum. "We have never been a violent family. Is it because of Vickie? Has she sparked some kind of violent streak in you that has been dormant this whole time? You know better than this, Alexis. Come on, now."

"Will you let me speak?"

She's right. Don't only lecture her. Hear her out. "Fine."

Alexis proceeded to explain the entire scenario—the hidden conversation, the setup, and why she attacked them. His anger subsided somewhat, although his frustration with her remained.

"I'm glad that you stood up for Vickie. I really am. And I'm grateful you were able to clear her name. Thank you for that. But you will still be punished. Other than work and school, you'll only see the inside of our house for the next two weeks. Do you understand?"

"Yeah."

He cracked a half-smile. "Still…thank you for watching out for her. But let's find a better way to do it next time, okay?"

Meanwhile, at school, Vickie had been called to the principal's office in the middle of the day, which sparked a sea of staring eyes that all clearly wondered why she was in trouble. She didn't know what to expect and her mind raced with possibilities.

Is this it? Will I be suspended for this lie that Megan and Abby told? Will I have any more chances to prove my innocence? What if I am expelled? Then what? I'm only now starting to feel like I'm at home in this school and I'll be kicked out.

To her relief, Mr Goede explained the situation and what had happened between Alexis, Megan, and Abby. He apologized to her that the mistake had been made and assured her that she was free and clear.

That evening, after track practice, she couldn't wait to get home and see Alexis. She dropped her bag at the top of the basement stairs and marched through the house to knock on her sister's bedroom door. Craig smiled as he pulled his jacket off and hung it on the hook near the door.

"You." Vickie walked into her room and pointed at Alexis. "You stood up for me."

"It was nothing." She rolled her eyes and shook her head. "Those girls were jerks. I was only in the right place at the right time."

She recounted the whole story of that morning, and the vampire was even more excited by the details. "You didn't even have to fight them. You could've simply walked away with the video."

"I know. That's what my dad and Mr Goede said. But I didn't feel like that was enough, you know? I wanted to punish them for what they were trying to do to you."

Vickie smiled warmly and gave her a hug. "I really appreciate it. Sometimes, I feel really alone in this world. You guys are great, but seeing you have my back like that means so much."

CHAPTER TWENTY-FIVE

Even though Vickie felt vindicated by the video Alexis took of her accusers and could now be free of at least one of the things she worried about, there were still other issues that occupied her mind.

The video of her damaging the car had gone viral and was shared over and over on social media. Still, she had little control over that situation and she merely vowed to keep her head down and to try not to spend too much of her brainpower thinking about it.

But that still left the matter of Eric's declaration of love. They hadn't gone on a date since the Festival dance, and whenever they saw each other at school, they made small talk. There were no meaningful conversations, and it worried her.

What Vickie didn't know was that he felt tortured over the situation, thinking that he'd ruined his relationship with her because he spoke about his feelings. Every night, he lay awake in his bed and wished he could go back in time to prevent himself from saying those words.

She wasn't sure what to hope for. While she was glad he had been honest with her about his feelings, she also felt enormous pressure over it—especially since it was explained to her that this was such a big deal.

While she lay on the sleeper sofa in the basement enjoying another VHS movie—this time, *Toy Story*—she thought constantly about how simple life had been in the old days. *The whole decision was made for you. Why do I always wish for something like that? It would be so much easier to go along with whatever my parents had decided for me. This is stupid.*

However, that thought also reminded her of her siblings' murder and how her last vision of the past resulted in her experiencing their final moments. Those images were burned into her memory and often, when she closed her eyes, she saw the cowering faces of her brother and sister again, waiting for the sword to end their lives.

Whenever she found herself going too far down that path, she shifted her mind quickly to the memory of Will destroying the members of the Circle who had hunted her in the present day. While it would never bring her siblings back, it at least calmed her to know that, even though she was the last true vampire, there were no vampire hunters looking to kill her people anymore.

Once again calmed by that fact, she thought of her parents. *They wanted to set me up with someone and that's also how they ended up together. It was simple and straightforward, and it made sense. Why wouldn't I want to be set up by two people who loved each other and had three children? My parents knew what they were doing.*

Then she remembered something her parents referenced before she was put to sleep. She sat on the sofa and paused the movie while she scanned her memory.

They talked about setting me up. My mother didn't want to put me to sleep because they wanted to arrange my marriage. They must have had someone in mind. But who? Who would have been my forever betrothed if I had stayed awake at that time?

Vickie turned the TV off entirely and closed her eyes. It was late that night, and other than the woman in the living room, everyone had gone to bed. She didn't have to worry about anyone interrupting her because at that point, Renee wouldn't get up from the recliner unless she wanted to stuff her face with popcorn or something.

She closed her eyes and took a few deep breaths. In her mind, she focused on her desire to see her parents.

When she opened her eyes, she stood in the middle of the castle foyer at the foot of the spiraling staircase. She smiled when she looked at the ornate chandelier hanging over her head. *I never get tired of coming back here. Ever. It's still home to me.*

Hearing voices coming from the kitchen area, she walked through the library and to where her parents sat together, eating a midday meal. Her father ripped pieces of bread in his hands and dipped them into a small bowl of soup in front of him. The smell was heavenly. *It must be some kind of chicken soup.*

For a moment, neither of the two spoke, but Vickie didn't care. She was in no rush and was content to stand there and enjoy the sight of her healthy, living parents sharing a meal. It was such a simple scene but one she hadn't seen for centuries.

Her father was the first one to say anything. "You're really that worried that Victoria is in town right now?"

"After what happened to the others, I will always be concerned about Victoria. Always." Her mother looked forlorn.

"Our dear daughter knows what she is doing. She only has to be aware of her surroundings. I told her to watch in all directions, and if she ever felt her powers leave her body, she should stay out in the open and in the most public area she can find. She will be safe."

But the man's wife was not convinced. "There is so much danger out there, my dear. Allowing her to be out there on her own is…irresponsible. We can't put her in that position."

While Vickie appreciated her mother's concern, she now remembered the specific instructions her father would give her before leaving. They were designed, she was told, to keep her safe in case of any surprise ambush by the Circle. He always assured her that the Circle wouldn't attack in a public area. It was strange how her subconscious had buried so many important memories.

"Let's speak of something happier," he insisted. "Let's talk about her marriage. Our little girl is now fourteen years old, and she is reaching marital age. She needs a suitor."

Her mother finished her bowl of soup and used her thumb to wipe a drip running down her chin. "I believe she would be best suited to Johann or Friedrich."

He smiled and nodded. "Johann was one of my final choices as well. I think they would be a lovely match together."

"Wonderful." She stood and carried her bowl to the counter. "I only hope she's alive for her marriage."

Her father drew his eyebrows together. "What is that supposed to mean?"

She hung her head and shook it. "You know what it means. They're coming for us. Already, they have taken our other two. Now, they want us and they want Vickie. They could be out there right now, hunting her, and we'd never know it. If they corner her at a place in the market and draw that horrible sword? She will be destroyed."

"No, she won't." He leaned back in his chair. "She's a responsible girl. She knows how to take care of herself. And if there is any risk, I will fetch her myself. Now, you think Johann is the perfect match for her?"

"I believe so." She nodded. "He would be a very fine man for her."

Vickie grimaced, grossed out by the suggestion. *Really? Johann was over a foot taller than me and several years older. We would have made a terrible couple.*

Of course, he had been a fellow vampire, so she would have no problem getting along with him. But the thought of being married to him?

The boy had been a family friend for as far back as Vickie knew. But she had vivid memories of him being considerably older than her. He was quiet, homely, and awkward.

I don't think Johann was unattractive but he somehow blended into the background. I would have died of boredom by our fifth anniversary. Come on, did you two really think this was my best chance at love?

"The important thing is that she would be taken care

of," her father continued. "Johann is a smart man and he would provide for her. I don't want her to marry anyone who might put her in the position where she would have to do all the work outside the house."

Her mother began cleaning the few dishes they used with a bucket of water she had filled from the pump. "Indeed. Victoria will be a fine wife, and Johann will be lucky to have her as well. I'm doing my best to teach her everything she needs to know so that she will be ready for marriage."

He placed his hands on her shoulders and kissed her on the cheek. "She has a wonderful example to follow."

While Vickie was warmed by this expression of affection between her parents, she still was stunned to hear that Johann had been her intended. She froze in the room and tried not to overreact or to speak to the images of the past as she had the tendency to do when searching her memories. She simply stood there, motionless, and watched them.

Her father walked to the table and sat again. "Of course, this all implies that we are able to get her to the marriage. I don't know how much more time we have."

"Is it even worth it?"

"We can't live our lives in fear. All we can do is hope that we will not be further victims of these attacks. We have our plans in place if we have to act, and we will take any steps that are necessary to protect our little girl. I won't let that happen again. But until our hand is forced, we must live normal lives. And that means planning for her future as a wife and mother."

She did the math in her head. *If I had stayed alive, I would probably have been married and with child by the time I was sixteen years old. And I would be living with Johann.*

Sadly, she shook her head at her parents' images and wished that this had been a happier memory to return to. But she was so terrified of the idea of being with Johann forever that she was struck again with grief. *I miss you both so much and yet, you would have secured my misery. I don't even know what to think about all this.*

Upset with feeling this way, she shook it off and returned to the present day and the basement where she opened her eyes on the sleeper sofa.

I have so much fun with Eric. What would have happened if I were fixed up with Johann? I would have none of the memories I have now—no fun times with Eric, our dates, our dances, our first kiss...all these things mean so much to me and they would be gone.

Vickie had no idea her feelings for Eric were that strong. She laid down, buried her face in her pillow, and wept. While she struggled to find a place in the current world, her old world would have forced her into a place she didn't want to be in.

CHAPTER TWENTY-SIX

The next night, Eric sat on the couch in his family's living room while his little sister watched *Frozen* on the TV. Yawning, he shook his head at her excitement while Elsa belted out *Let It Go* for the hundredth time.

I can't believe how many times she's seen this. "Don't you ever get tired of this movie, Amber?"

She, however, paid no attention to him at all. She bounced around the room, dancing and spinning around while she sang, "Let it goooo, let it gooooo! Can't hold it back anymoooore!"

Annoyed and amused at the same time, Eric pulled his phone out and unlocked it. *No email. Nothing new going on in Facebook. It looks like a quiet night. Maybe there's something on YouTube I can watch.* He'd no sooner tapped on the YouTube icon when his phone dinged with a new message from Vickie.

Please be good. Please be good. Please be good. Please be good. He chanted this in his head every time a new message came in from Vickie. He had been literally crippled with fear that whenever she contacted him, it would be to break up with him.

He opened the messaging app and saw three simple words.

Vickie: what's your address?

It was an odd question and one that gave him a moment's hesitation. Eric had never given her his address. He thought his family was weird and he didn't really want her to meet them. While he tolerated his mother—who was generally sweet—his sister was embarrassing and his father had a temper. In the interest of protecting the relationship, he kept their hangouts to places outside of his house, like Johnny V's.

Eric: Why?

Vickie: I need to see you right now

This wasn't really an answer he wanted to see and now, his mind was filled with all the reasons why she would want to see him right now. *Does she want to break up with me? That has to be it. This is finally happening. She wants to break up with me and doesn't want to do it over the phone. I knew this was too good to last. We were going to break up eventually. My dad even said that high school girlfriends never last.*

Eric: What do you need to see me about? Can't you say it here?

Vickie: no

Vickie: send me your address

Eric: Is it bad?

Vickie: It's not something I want to say on here. I want to say it in person

Eric: You have a ride?

Vickie: trust me. What's your address?

Eric took a deep breath. He wasn't concerned about his family embarrassing him now. All he cared about was why she wanted to come over. He wasn't protecting his address at that moment because of what she might learn about him. He was keeping it quiet because he wanted to delay what seemed inevitable.

As long as you wait, it's only going to get worse. If she has to do this in person, you'd rather have her do it here than do it at school in front of people. Give it to her and rip the Band-Aid off as quickly as you can.

Eric: 4203 Elmbrook Court

Vickie: Okay. Thanks. I'm nearby so I won't be very long

He wasn't sure if that was a good thing or a bad thing, but he paced around the house while he waited for her. *I should have never told her I loved her. This is it. I ruined something amazing because I couldn't keep my mouth shut. Now, it's all over.*

A lump formed uncomfortably in his throat while he watched for her out the window. He didn't even know what he would be watching for—a car?

Vickie, of course, wasn't nearby. She was at home, highlighted his address, and searched for it before she pulled up a map with directions from her house. Once it appeared on her screen, she scanned it and committed it to memory.

She stood, walked upstairs, and knocked on Alexis' door before she poked her head in. "Hey. Do you have a sec?"

Her sister chuckled at the question. "I have an abundance of them, yes. I'm grounded, remember?"

The vampire stepped in. "Right. Well, I only wanted to be polite. Listen, I need you to do me a favor."

"It would be more than whatever it is I'm doing now." She closed the magazine in front of her. "What's up?"

"Can you run interference for me? I need to sneak out."

Alexis tilted her head. "Why? Where are you going? Should I be worried?"

"No, but I don't have time to set up a ride or anything like that. I have to go." She bounced anxiously on her heels.

"Vickie, if you're going out to save puppies, smash cars, or whatever—"

She dragged her fingertips down her face in frustration. "I'm not going out to do vampire stuff. I will use my speed, but you know no one can see me when I do that if I'm careful."

"If you're careful." The other girl rolled her eyes. "Come on, Dad is already terrified you'll use your powers in public more and get yourself caught. Do you really want to risk that?"

Vickie bit her lip. "Yeah, this time I do."

"Where are you going?" Alexis sighed.

"Eric's. I need to talk to him for a few minutes. Make up some reason why I'm not here if your dad asks."

"You're getting a little too bold. If you aren't here, he will ask way too many questions. I can lie for you, but I don't know how many lies I can tell in a row."

A little desperate now, she put her hands on her hips and stared out the window while she wracked her brains for a good plan. *How can I get out of here?* "I have it. Tell him

I'm sleeping. Say I've had a long day and I decided to go to bed. He won't check on me and he'll stay out of the basement. It's perfect."

"Fine. Don't be late."

She walked out the side door and down to the foot of the driveway. Her sister watched from her bedroom window as she closed her eyes and recalled the map she'd memorized, planning her route. When the energy filled her arms and legs, she blurred into motion.

When she vanished from view, Alexis hoped quietly that she knew what she was doing—and that she'd get there and back without incident.

About an hour later, Craig walked in the door and she met him in the kitchen. "Hey, Dad, Vickie asked if you could keep it down when you got home tonight."

He glanced at the basement door. "Why?"

"Because she's gone to bed already. Apparently, she had a long day today so she zonked out early."

"Oh. I hope she's okay."

Yeah, me too. "I think she is. She looked tired, though."

Her father bought it and chose to speak quietly and keep the TV volume low to be respectful to Vickie—which made his daughter really feel bad because he had no clue she wasn't home.

On the other side of town, the vampire stopped at the corner of Elmbrook Court and Holy Hill Road and took a moment to run her fingers through her hair. No one was on that corner and she could walk confidently down Elmbrook to Eric's house without suspicion.

He felt like his heart stopped when he saw her turn the corner. *Did she walk here? She really needed to see you this badly? That is never a good sign, man.* He walked warily outside into the somewhat chilly air and stood in the middle of the driveway, his arms at his sides, and watched her approach the house. His eyes were wide and he was nervous, but he simply waited for her to walk up to him.

For once, he didn't say a word. She could tell he probably waited for the other shoe to drop and so walked right up to him in the driveway and held both her hands out. He took them cautiously but still didn't speak.

"Things have been weird between us for a while."

Tears welled up in his eyes. *Oh, man, here we go.* "I know they have."

She nodded. "That's my fault. See, when you told me you loved me, I didn't know how to react. I didn't know what to say or what that even meant. You opened your heart to me, and I froze."

"That's okay." His voice shook while he searched desperately for the right response. "I didn't expect you to say anything." That was a lie, of course. He always wanted to hear her say it but had convinced himself it wasn't a big deal.

Vickie shook her head. "Where I come from, love is a very different thing. It's something you develop. You're kinda forced into it and have to learn it. That's what I was used to. I was expected to love who I was told to love, rather than allow myself to fall in love with someone else."

Eric took a deep breath. "Vickie, do what you came

here to do. Please." He wanted this over with. It was killing him.

She looked at their hands—their fingers intertwined—and back at him. "I love you too, Eric." She leaned in and kissed him.

A rush of warmth washed over him. He couldn't believe what he had heard. "Are you serious?"

"I am more serious about this than anything. Revisiting some of those memories reminded me of how much I care about you and how much I want to be with you and only you. I'm sorry it took me so long to realize it, but I love you."

He embraced her and breathed a sigh of relief. "I don't care how long it took, I'm so happy to hear you say it at all."

They stayed and talked for a few minutes while they stared at each other with permanent smiles on their faces. But eventually, she realized it was getting too late. "I have to go."

"Okay. Thanks for coming by. I normally don't like it when people visit my house but I'm willing to make that exception for you."

She smiled and laughed. "I love you."

"I love you too."

After one more deep, passionate kiss, she turned and headed to the sidewalk. She turned right, smiled at him one more time, and walked down the road until she was out of sight.

Once she was in the clear, she smiled to herself, danced an excited jig on the sidewalk, and engaged her super-speed to sprint home. She stopped in front of the house and saw the living room light on.

Carefully, Vickie crept through the yard and peeked into the window. The two adults were seated in their chairs, Craig looking miserable as the local news was on the TV again. To her relief, Alexis' light was on, too.

She walked furtively to the window and tapped on it a few times until the other girl answered her. "Fancy meeting you here."

"Knock it off. Can you let me in the side door?"

Her sister shook her head. "Okay, but then I'm done doing you favors for a while. Make sure they don't see you in the living room window."

"Don't worry."

Alexis tried to stroll casually past the living room and through the kitchen, where she coughed loudly to cover up the sound of the side door unlocking. She eased the door open enough for the vampire to slip through and go directly into the basement. With another loud cough, she managed to close and lock the side door again.

At the bottom of the stairs, Vickie turned the light on and smiled. *You pulled it off, girl.* She opened her laptop to see a message waiting from Eric, which was simply a heart emoji.

The other girl filled a glass of water and carried it back to her room as an excuse to be walking around. She smiled at the two adults seated in the living room and disappeared into her bedroom. *Getting into fistfights and running interference for people sneaking out of the house—boy, Alexis, you've really changed these days.*

CHAPTER TWENTY-SEVEN

That Friday night was filled with a different kind of energy in the household.

Vickie was dancing on air, of course, after professing her love to her boyfriend. Alexis was surprisingly chipper, although she still had to carry out her sentence for the fight at school. Craig whistled in carefree fashion while he made dinner, even though he was still unsuccessful on the dating scene.

The day had been rainy, dreary, and unseasonably cold again. There was nothing on TV but reruns and no one had plans.

But it was the last day Aunt Renee would be at the house. After dinner, she would take Lucky and head off to Tomahawk.

The family was elated. While she had spent time going through many of Carol's old items, the trade-off was brutal. She had annoyed everyone, invaded their personal space, taken the house over, and generally inconvenienced them all. The girls resorted to spending all their free time hidden in their bedrooms—or, in Vickie's case, the basement.

Craig heated a pan of spaghetti sauce while the noodles finished cooking. He tossed a bag of broccoli in the microwave to steam. A few minutes later, dinner was on the table, and the four of them sat and ate.

Previous family dinners had been quiet, somber affairs, as Renee dominated the conversations and steered them all to something about herself, including such attractive topics as incontinence and skin abnormalities.

She took full opportunity of the last dinner together to lecture him on his dating efforts.

"First of all, you don't need to be dating anyone right now." She paused to chew her food and swallow. "You are still grieving, obviously. That's not fair to your wife, and it's not fair to these poor women who have to deal with your grief as well. There's absolutely no need for this. You should take your time and date when it comes naturally to you, not by going out and finding women on the Internet. What would Carol say to that? I can't imagine my sister going online to find a man. I think she'd be ashamed of you. And your daughter? Alexis is desperate for her father to be here for her. You can't shirk that responsibility simply because you're lonely."

This lecture went on and on. He took it with good humor, smiled politely at her, and ate in silence. *She'll be gone in about an hour. Her car is already packed and ready to go. All you need to do is get through this dinner and you can send her on her way.*

Once he finished his meal, he dabbed his mouth with a napkin and swallowed the last mouthful. "Oh, I almost forgot. I think there's one more box in the basement you wanted to take with you. Let me check."

The girls smirked at each other, both knowing it was simply an excuse to escape the dinner early. But they both were also encouraged by the fact that the clock was ticking and Renee would be gone before they knew it.

Craig reached the bottom of the stairs and glanced at the living area, where Vickie had been sleeping for a month. *Poor girl. She'll be so happy to be in her own bedroom again.* He walked past it and opened the laundry room door, yanked the pull chain, and turned the light on.

When the glow of the bulb illuminated the space, he stopped and stared at the storage area. It was once overrun by boxes from floor to ceiling. Now, there was only a neatly stacked pile of boxes against the far wall.

I'll give her grief for making us miserable this month, but Renee sure did help to go through all this stuff. Wow. We made more progress than I thought.

Sure enough, there was a box on the floor that was labeled, *CAROL TOYS*. Inside it were old Barbie dolls and plush toys from her childhood. Craig had no emotional attachment to them, but Renee insisted they not be thrown out. In response, he'd told her she had to take them with her.

He retrieved the box, turned the light off, and jogged up the steps. Back in the kitchen, he placed it on the counter and nodded to Renee. "I'll help you get this one in the car in a few minutes. It's only some old toys—Barbies and whatever else."

Renee smiled while she cut some of the spaghetti noodles with the side of her fork. "You know, Alexis, your mom and I used to play Barbies every day when we were kids. But she loved to organize so much that she only wanted to set up the Dream House—put the shoes away, put the clothes away, put the TV over here and the couch over there…she absolutely loved it. Whenever we sat down to play, it was always something like Barbie Moves Into Her New House or whatever. She'd pretend to move in and set her home up, and that was the whole game. Oh, Carol loved to organize."

Craig sat at the table and folded his hands with a smile. "Yes, she did. Carol was very organized. It was one of the many reasons why I loved her."

The woman looked at her plate of food and her lip began to quiver. She set the fork down on her plate and covered her mouth before tears began to stream down her cheeks. Quietly, she sobbed while the rest of the family watched her awkwardly.

"Are you okay, Renee?" he asked her after a long while.

"I only… I miss my sister so much." She tried to hold it together but a few sobs burst out behind her hands.

He stood and walked over to her side of the table to place his hand on her shoulder. "Hey, Renee, it's okay. I miss her too."

"Me too, Aunt Renee." Alexis tried to sound encouraging. "I think about her every day."

"Yeah. This house is full of her memories. She's always here." He rubbed her shoulder. "You don't have to torture yourself like that."

Renee tried to compose herself. "It's actually why I came here. I wanted to be closer to her again, even if only for a little while. Her spirit is still alive and well, and I thought I could take a few of her things back with me, too."

Craig returned to the seat on the other side of the table. "You came here and spent a month living in this house only to be closer to your sister again?"

She sniffed loudly. "I thought it would feel like it was the same again. Like when I used to come here with Mom and visit for Christmas. I thought it would be nice, like old times. But I guess Mom was right."

Confused, he shook his head. "What do you mean by that?"

"I wanted Mom to come too. I thought if she did, it would really feel like old times again. But she didn't want to come. She said it would be too hard for her. In her mind, all of you have moved on but I didn't want to believe that."

"Renee, you had to have known that we wouldn't spend an entire month talking about Carol anymore. We all think about her, but we can't focus on the fact that she's gone all the time. It would bury us in so much grief, we wouldn't be able to get out of bed in the morning. Carol wouldn't want that. She loved seeing us happy—and she loved seeing you happy too."

Alexis nodded. "We have moved on, Aunt Renee. But Mom is still here. She's just not *here*."

Renee leaned over and touched Alexis' cheek. "You know something? One of the best parts of being here has been seeing you. You look so much like your mother, you have no idea. Simply looking at you reminds me that her spirit is alive."

"You know something, Renee?" He took his daughter's

hand and squeezed it gently. "I think so too. She's the spitting image of her mother."

"I only wish this wasn't so hard." Renee sniffed again and returned to her noodles. "Up in Tomahawk, it's only me and Mom. We have such a hard time some days, and it's not like we saw Carol all the time. Just knowing that she's not here is hard enough and there's no one there to really comfort us."

Everyone nodded politely. The woman was boorish but she had kicked it into overdrive while she was there because she was so focused on her sister. She struggled with the same grief they had but unlike them, she had no outlet for it.

"Renee, me trying to date again has nothing to do with Carol. It has to do with me moving forward. Carol is still in my heart and always will be. There is a place there that only she could ever fill. But she's gone now. I'm not married anymore."

Alexis nodded. "Yeah, Aunt Renee. My dad talked to me about dating before he decided to do it. I told him to do it. I want to see him happy too. I know he still cares about my mom. But he's right—she's not here anymore."

"How do you all deal with that?" Renee stabbed a stalk of broccoli with her fork. "How can you talk about her being gone and not be totally wrecked with pain and anguish all the time?"

Craig pointed to a picture of a rooster hanging on the kitchen wall. "Do you see that rooster, Renee? I hate that thing. It's ugly, it looks kinda tacky, and it doesn't fit with the rest of the kitchen. When Carol came home with that one day, I wanted to throw it in the dumpster. But she insisted on it, so we kept it. Now that she's gone, I wouldn't dare think of throwing it out. It's this friendly little reminder of good times that I want to keep in front of me."

His daughter decided to jump in as well. "That's right. And I have my own stuff from Mom. I have an old piggy bank she had when she was a little girl. She gave me a pair of earrings once that I wear almost every day." She pulled back her hair to reveal a pair of diamond earrings. "You find ways to think about the good times with Mom and then, you go about your day."

He nodded, always so proud of how his daughter handled her grief. "You can't deny the hurt or bury it. It's okay to feel it. But think about the good times and move forward. You have to. And fortunately, you have a trunk full of memories you get to take home with you. I'm sure you and your mom will be able to find some ways to keep Carol's memory alive in your day-to-day life too."

After dinner, he shoved the last box into the overflowing back seat of Renee's car and opened the door for Lucky to jump in. The dog was as excited to go home as the family was to finally get rid of him.

Renee gave warm hugs and kisses to both girls—even though Vickie hardly knew her—and gave Craig a big squeeze. "You're a good man, and you're honoring my sister the right way."

"Drive safe, Renee."

She wedged herself into her car, gave a final wave, and drove off on a three-and-a-half-hour trip to Tomahawk. The group collectively breathed a sigh of relief before Vickie raced downstairs to retrieve her things and move back into her bedroom.

"Aunt Renee's really hurting, huh, Dad?"

He put his arm around his daughter. "She really is. And that's okay. She's doing her best, but unfortunately, so much of her bad behavior seems to be amplified because of your mom's passing. She's not a bad person deep down but has some questionable character traits, that's all."

With a triumphant smile, the vampire strutted through the kitchen with a bag over her shoulder and a pillow tucked under her arm while her family shared a chuckle over her excitement.

CHAPTER TWENTY-EIGHT

It was a Monday morning, and the girls practically skipped off to school. They had a peaceful weekend—no one made plans, even though the girls had boys who were interested in them and Craig wanted to go on more dates.

Instead, they deliberately stayed home and enjoyed having full control over the house again. The girls lounged in the living room simply because they could, and he spent most of the time watching old episodes of *The Office* and *The Simpsons*— another show Renee obdurately refused to watch.

It was a gloriously lazy weekend. Now, the girls were out the door and on their way back to school and he stood in the middle of his house—home alone for the first time in a month.

He turned the music on and washed the breakfast dishes. With everything clean and packed away, he poured himself a cup of coffee and wandered down the hall to his room. He had recorded episodes of the podcast while

Renee was there but had to give her explicit instructions to stay quiet—a request that was either overlooked by her or flat-out ignored by her dog.

Despite the heavy editing that was necessary for those episodes, he managed to keep up with his publishing schedule. Now that things were back to normal, he could even record with the bedroom door open. There would be no interruptions, thank goodness.

As he assembled his notes for the day's episode, he chuckled to himself while he relived the failed dates he had found through MatchMe. The entire experience could have been enough to turn him off dating entirely, but he knew that it was purely a temporary setback and that MatchMe was probably not the right approach for him.

Craig plugged his microphone in, flipped his laptop open, and pressed the big, red *RECORD* button.

"Hello, and welcome to another edition of *The Truth About...* a podcast series that dives deeper than the headlines to uncover the personal realities and unspoken facts about the things you thought you knew. I'm your host, Craig Watson, former journalist and investigative reporter.

"Normally, on this show, I like to talk to my daughter and my adopted daughter, and we speak about the realities of our new lives together and the complications therein. Today, I'll go solo to get really personal with you all on a topic that may strike close to home for many—dating.

"But before we get into that, I'd like to take a brief moment to tell you about the SquidPillow."

He was awash in free products and sponsored items, and the SquidPillow had been one of his favorites—a customizable pillow that was tailored to your physical needs and how you slept. It was his new favorite perk and he loved recording commercials for it.

"Now, on with the show.

"There are three major pieces of advice I want to share with you about dating. I've dipped my toes in the dating pool again. It's been about a year since my wife passed away and I felt it was time to start at least considering romance again.

"Before I did so, I sat down and talked to my daughter about it. I didn't want her to feel like I was offending her or disrespecting her mother's memory. The fact is, as much as it still hurts at times, my wife is gone and I have to move forward. She didn't like seeing me in pain when she was alive, so there is no sense in continuing to be in pain now.

"My daughter, bless her heart, was immediately supportive of the decision to go back to dating, and she has been my number-one fan throughout this process. Having support behind you while going through something like this is very important, and I don't think I would even attempt to do this if she wasn't on board. I'm thankful that she is.

"I signed up with an online dating service—and no, I won't go into any details on which service I used, as I don't want this to be a critique of dating services in general or even a critique of this particular app. It might work very well for many but I can't honestly say it worked very well for me. But that's beside the point.

"The first thing I learned about dating in this day and age is that it is something of a minefield. You have to be careful where you step because disaster can strike at any time. In my case, disaster struck three times in one weekend, but I digress.

"I thought dating would be fun like it was in high school. I assumed early dates would be casual and enjoyable but to be frank, they sometimes felt like job interviews. I was so worried about what I would say, or what my date would say, that I couldn't simply relax and enjoy the process, which is what you're supposed to do when you go out on a date.

"Those metaphorical mines can reveal themselves in any number of concerning ways. Some people move too fast, others too slow, and others might merely have a personality that clashes with your own."

In this portion of the episode, Craig recounted in detail his three dates from the disaster-filled weekend—the one with zero manners, the one who seemed to flirt with anything that moved, and the one who was so competitive she couldn't be fun to be around.

"The moral of the story—other than 'don't schedule three dates in a row for yourself'—is simple. There are innumerable fish in the sea and many of them are a terrible fit for you. Be prepared to be frustrated but don't let it get you down."

Then, he thought about the constant comments he heard about his wife from Renee and how they made him feel. And he even thought about the woman he'd met at the podcast conference who flirted with him.

"But I will tell you this—the hardest part of dating for me is the guilt.

"I shouldn't feel guilty and part of me accepts that. I know my wife would approve of me dating again. My daughter already approves. But there's this weird, icky feeling when you re-enter the dating scene after having been married for a long time.

"I committed myself to my wife, through sickness and in health, and spent decades with her. Being on a date with someone else often simply feels wrong.

"And in order to get past that feeling and get on with your date, you have to do something that might feel impossible. You have to ignore it.

"Ignore the guilt. If you feel ready to date again, you should. And if you can't ignore the guilt, you're not ready to date. I can't eliminate that guilty feeling. But ignoring it until I feel better is okay with me. If I can't shake it after I've made the effort, I have to stop.

"I think this is universal for people in my position. Your marriage didn't end because you chose to end it. You're not someone who went through a divorce. Your spouse was taken from you. And that's a subtle difference but it's an important one. You didn't stop loving your spouse. They stopped living.

"Your love continues, however, and it will always have a piece of your heart. But if you're interested in dating again, you have to accept that fact."

It was the hardest thing that Craig had to deal with as he worked his way through dating. His vision of Carol assuring him he would be okay and that she approved definitely helped. But exactly as he had often doubted her whenever she said things like that while she was alive, he sometimes didn't quite believe her when she told him he could date again.

The last piece of advice was the most important and one he struggled to follow.

"My daughter has recently found what appears to be a boyfriend. I say 'appears' because I can't keep up with how kids date these days. I think they're dating. They went to a dance together, and she seems to be really into him, but that's not the point I'm making.

"Before they got together, she came to me, frustrated that she was lonely and wanted to date but had a hard time seeing any boy going out with her. I don't think I'm embarrassing her when I say that because so many girls go through it. Shoot, so many guys do, too!

"When she talked to me about it, I gave her two simple truths about dating that I had learned over the years.

"One, there's someone out there right now who likes you and you can't be closed off to those opportunities. Often, they are right under your nose."

He recounted the story of Katie in high school and their mutual crush that never went anywhere.

"And two, you shouldn't try so hard.

"This is probably the hardest piece of advice I struggle to follow myself. After all, there are numerous times when I try to 'force' it. I did it that weekend when I went on all those dates.

"The most important truth to follow is that dating really has changed since we went to high school. If you are on a date with someone, you don't have to try to earn their interest anymore. You already have it. Relax and be yourself, and the chips will fall wherever they fall.

"As a classic overthinker, I've struggled with that one."

He wrapped the podcast episode up telling a few stories

about how nervous he used to be on dates and why he tried too hard to impress girls—which never led to anything positive.

Finally, he closed the episode.

"As many of you know, this podcast digs deep into what's under the surface of the things in the world. Mixed families are a huge part of that because there's so much that you can dig into.

"You might be tempted to think this is simply a throw-away episode and that you have nothing to learn from some guy trying to date again.

"But if you take the time to pay attention here, you might be surprised. The most fascinating and useful things to uncover are often personal and emotional.

"This is how dating has been for me so far, and I have a feeling that many of you are going through the same thing. Sometimes, simply knowing that fact is enough to keep you going because you are not alone in your struggles.

"I'll see you next time on *The Truth About...*"

It was a solid if unspectacular episode. But getting personal had always done well in the numbers and the episodes he'd thought would be home runs often disappointed in the ratings.

A week later, when the episode went live, it became one of the top three episodes he ever produced. The people still enjoyed hearing the personal struggles and speaking them out loud was therapeutic for him.

Now, he merely hoped he could find a normal date.

CHAPTER TWENTY-NINE

Eric sat in his room on his laptop, completely disinterested in listening to *Let It Go* for at least the one hundred and seventh time.

As he scrolled through Facebook, an open window displayed a casual chat with Vickie.

Eric: I wish you could randomly show up to my house more often!

Vickie: Anytime!

Eric: Well, maybe someday. I like having you over but I really don't want my family to embarrass me

Vickie: Aw, how bad could they be?

Eric: You'd be surprised

This conversation rolled on, and the two bantered between them and discussed the week's events at school. Vickie confided the story of Megan and Abby and how they had conspired to set her up, which made him angry.

But it was a typical night, otherwise, and the young couple simply kept each other company from afar.

As he scrolled through Facebook, Eric clicked on videos

that came up to pass the time between responses in his conversation. He watched a cat playing piano and a couple of kids lip-syncing to death metal. Some were amusing while others were merely a waste of his time.

Finally, he stumbled on a different video titled, *YOU WON'T BELIEVE YOUR EYES!!!*

He was always skeptical of these overhyped headlines but he clicked on it anyway since he had nothing better to do.

At first, he frowned as he watched a traffic video in which a car barreled down the road, headed toward a puppy standing in an intersection. He winced and almost stopped the video, worried that this would be some kind of gore video of a dog being hit by a car. *This kind of thing isn't my style. Oh please, don't hit the dog.*

To his utter amazement, a figure entered the frame from the side. The video was black-and-white, but a skinny person in a hooded sweatshirt literally sprinted towards the car. With no apparent hesitation, it struck the front of the vehicle and caused significant damage.

Wow, that's a cool effect. It looked almost real. These so-called found footage things are so cheesy but they did this one really well. I wonder who did it.

Abruptly, the video switched to color footage from a cell phone. The man recording the incident rambled in the background but the shot zoomed in on the hooded figure. Thanks to the color, he could see the sweatshirt was pink and, when he squinted, he realized it said *Clear Lake High School* on the shirt.

Did...did someone from school make this video? No one has those kinds of resources, do they? Not at our school, anyway.

Vickie: I have to go. I love you!

Eric: I love you too babe. Sleep good

He closed the chat window and returned to the video, now completely transfixed by it.

That hoodie looks familiar, too.

Eric watched the rest of the video, which included a news interview with the man who had filmed it on his cell phone. It was the same footage Craig had seen on the local news, describing the incident and his reaction to it.

At first, he was still convinced it was a scam. *There's absolutely no way this kind of thing could happen in real life. Come on, now. But why would they go through the trouble of putting a Clear Lake sweatshirt on it? Is this one of those weird things where it's tailored to my device? Like, the bot knows I'm from Clear Lake so they edit the video automatically? Do the kids who go to Hartford High School see a different version of this video?*

The questions swirled in his head and he scrolled to the hundreds of comments attached to the video, knowing that he had leapt into a rabbit hole that would consume the rest of his night.

Various comments claimed the video was fake and doctored and pointed out little imperfections in each video that, according to the skeptics, were proof that it never happened. Still, many believers hung out in the comments section and peppered the conversation with various conspiracy theories and other assorted thoughts.

One comment stood out.

I was there. That's me in the video talking to the news crew.

Eric clicked on the guy's profile picture. Sure enough, his picture matched with the man in the video. He scanned through the comments to see what he had to say, and he came across this description.

It was a girl. She couldn't have been more than high school age, or at least she looked really young. But it was definitely a girl with her face and hair tucked into the hoodie. She was really skittish when I approached, and she wouldn't answer anything I had to say. Instead, she ran off in the other direction. I tried to keep up with her, but she ducked into another street and disappeared. You can see that in the full video (I attached it below). The news crew cuts out the chase footage, but it's there. I've never experienced anything like this. I couldn't sleep for days afterward.

He clicked on the attached video and watched as the girl in the hoodie ran away from the camera. When he paused it and maximized it to full screen to get a better look, his stomach sank.

That's a Clear Lake High School Cross Country hoodie. It... that can't be, right?

His mind raced as he checked the timestamp of the video and when the whole accident was claimed to have taken place. He opened Vickie's Facebook profile and clicked on her photos.

If this is her, she would be wearing the outfit in other pictures that day, right? If there are any pictures from that day on Facebook, she'll be in that pink sweatshirt.

For a moment, he wondered why no one from the high school had looked at this video more closely. But then again, he also knew he had a tendency to look more closely at things than others did. Maybe they breezed past it casually and simply moved on. But his need for answers usually fed his curiosity.

He scrolled through the pictures until he reached a handful of photos from an indoor track meet that was held on the same day as the alleged accident. To his shock, he saw a photo of Vickie and Krista—and Vickie wore the hoodie. She also wore black breakaway pants, which matched the pants in the video.

Eric covered his mouth, which now hung open. *Vickie is the girl in the video? There's... Wait...no, that can't be. Unless it's part of some kind of project she was working on or she was simply part of some prank?*

Frantically, he opened a chat window and pinged Vickie, hoping she would still be awake.

Eric: Hey

Eric: Are you up?

Eric: I have to ask you something. It's nothing bad, I promise

Eric: Call me when you wake up tomorrow

Eric: I don't want to be weird, but I saw this video online that looks like you and it's really confusing me

He closed his laptop. *She must be sleeping. I hope she's not too annoyed by all the notifications.*

Unable to settle, he placed the laptop on his bed beside him and played the video again. Nothing about it made sense. *She comes out of nowhere. She crashes into the car and destroys it but doesn't have a scratch on her. And this is an intersection very close to school. I can't get a good look at the face but that has to be her, doesn't it?*

He had enormous difficulty falling asleep that night. As he stared at the ceiling, he kept replaying the footage in his head, over and over again. *Does she have some kind of weird superpower? No, that's stupid. But is it? Is she a superhero or an alien or something? I know her, but I don't know her that well.*

How much does she talk about her childhood or her past? Not much, right?

As he continued down this line of thought, he began to reframe other experiences with her, especially a recent one.

She never told me how she got to my house. How did she get there? Did she walk? Or run? That doesn't make any sense. But think about all the things you don't know about the girl you love. She could be hiding something. But what?

The next morning, Vickie woke and saw she had five notifications from Eric. With a bright smile, she unlocked her phone. *He is such a sweet boy. It's probably a flurry of love notes or something adorable like that. I'm really enjoying this love thing.*

She couldn't imagine swapping love notes with Johann.

But when she saw what the notifications were, she froze. Eric was asking way too many questions, and the video that went public might have finally caught up to her.

Shoot. What do I do? Do I tell Craig and Alexis? What will they think? Or can I make something up to get out of this? I can't tell Eric that I'm a vampire—he'll either think I'm crazy or he'll run away screaming.

Will I have to reveal myself to him? And if so, what happens then?

CHAPTER THIRTY

Jim Trembo sat with his colleague in the conference room of the hotel. Pete Stabone practically bounced with energy.

"Geez, Pete." He shook his head. "You look like I did the other day when we got the test results in. What's up?"

The man smiled. "Jim, I feel like you did the other day. I've been a believer of yours for a while now. I wouldn't be here, with my family back home, if I didn't believe in what we were doing."

He nodded slowly. "Okay. It sounds like you're setting me up here, Pete."

Pete pulled his laptop out. "I'm not saying I doubted you, Jim, but I've spent this whole time not thoroughly convinced that we could get this thing across the finish line."

This was news to him. "You're telling me that you didn't think we could turn this investigation into anything credible? You saw the test results and you still weren't convinced?"

His companion closed his eyes and shrugged sheepishly. "I'm not defending it, Jim. It's simply where we are. I've seen too many of these projects end up in dead ends. I know your history. I know how even the surest of things can wind up faltering."

Jim leaned back in his chair and folded his arms. "Pete, are you quitting now? Why are we down here?"

With a devilish grin, Pete flipped his laptop open, pressed play on a video, and spun it so the screen faced the other man. On the video, a hooded figure crashed into a car and inflicted significant damage.

He nodded, confused. "It looks good. I like it. And it's very well done. Did you do this, Pete? Are you looking for feedback?"

The other man's mouth dropped open. "What?"

"You're showing me some kind of computer-generated video, right? What is this, CGI? It can't be practical effects, can it? It looks very real."

Pete laughed in disbelief. "You, of all people, haven't seen this video?"

"Not really. I've been deep into all this stuff, researching the Circle. I haven't had time for web videos."

He grabbed Jim's arm and squeezed it tightly. "Jim. This is a real video from a traffic camera a few weeks ago. The intersection where it was filmed was not far from here at all."

Jim almost looked disappointed in his colleague. "Pete, come on. You're not going to fall for this, are you? They can plaster people faces onto other videos and make them look convincing. It's called deep-fakes. That's more impressive than this video. This is only a poor-quality Photoshop job…or whatever they use to edit video."

"Think about it!" He slapped his palm on the table. "This is located in Milwaukee. Jim, we're here investigating supernatural activity in Milwaukee. Who would fake this and set it in Milwaukee at the same time we're closing in on a supernatural investigation in the same area?"

His superior leaned forward and watched the video again. "Who sent you this?"

"Everyone. This is a popular video online right now. It's getting news coverage because it's coming from the real deal. This feed was presented by the Milwaukee Police Department." Pete's eyes grew wider with every sentence. "Jim—this is the supernatural activity we're looking for. This is the smoking gun. It's the proof we need. If there is truly a supernatural presence in Milwaukee, Wisconsin, it's coming from this person. This being…whatever."

Jim took a deep breath and ran his fingers through his hair while he rocked slowly and thoughtfully in the chair. "Play it again."

Pete tapped on his trackpad and started the video. Then, on Jim's orders, he paused it. Jim pointed to the screen. "See right there? What does that say? Zoom in."

He squinted. "It says *Clear Lake High School.*"

"So a student from Clear Lake High School inflicted that kind of damage on a car and came out unscathed. It looks like a female student, too." Still, he twisted his face in confusion. "I don't know. We're finding evidence of some kind of creature that has been hunted by a religious group based out of Austria for centuries, culminating in an apparent bloody battle in a random field in the middle of Milwaukee…and that creature is a high school girl? How does a being like that even get into high school? And where do we go from here?"

Pete closed the laptop. "We go to the high school."

"And ask them, 'Hey, do you have any weird inhuman creatures on your roster?' We'll have to find this person somehow and watch them from a distance. Frequenting high school girls' sports as a couple of guys with no students at the school could quickly look creepy."

"We can work out the details later." The other man waved his hand dismissively. "But look, this is meant to be, man. It's all coming together and better than it ever has. We have real, documented presence of something insane happening, and we can tie it to the work that we're doing."

"A high school girl," Jim muttered constantly to himself. "There's clearly an element of speed to this, along with some kind of either indestructibility or healing powers that this creature has tapped into. How do you do that much damage to a car and not be hurt yourself?"

Pete shrugged. "We have more questions than answers right now, that's for sure. But we have something. This is progress. Serious progress. We can turn this into so much more. If we can somehow tie this video to the creatures we're uncovering in the field, we have a home run."

"Vampires."

"Huh?"

"It's vampires. The Circle hunted vampires a few hundred years ago. They used that sword to murder vampires. So that's the kind of creature we're dealing with here."

The other man grew even more excited. "So, if we can tie vampires to the abilities present in this video, the game is over. We can zero in on her, get her in our grasp, and you can put her to work the way you always wanted. You can fundamentally transform this country's military efforts—maybe even law enforcement. A whole race of indestructible vampires."

Now, Jim grew more excited as well. "Can you imagine how quickly laws would be followed in America? You can't outrun the cops, you can't stop them, and you can't hurt them. They will keep everyone in line."

Almost rigid in his chair with enthusiasm, Pete joined in the daydream. "We could control the world with an army of creatures that need no special equipment. They could charge at a firing opponent and walk through whatever they shoot." He looked at his watch. "I have a call, so I'll go upstairs. But we need to keep working on this. Jim, your ship has finally come in. We'll find this creature and get our hands on it."

He stood and left the room, leaving his colleague alone at the table. Jim was excited but also very cautious. It seemed too good to be true. He stood and walked over to the window to stare out at the mall across the street.

A high school girl? Does my entire career and legacy come down to tracking and bringing in a high school girl? It can't be falling into place this easily.

But who am I to argue with evidence? Maybe it's time I start learning a little more about these vampires—and getting my foot into Clear Lake High School.

The adventures and challenges don't end here. The Agency is getting closer. Vickie has to learn how to get by without using her powers. Follow Vicki, Alexis and Craig's journey in <u>The Girl Retreats.</u>

Get sneak peeks, exclusive giveaways, behind the scenes content, and more.
PLUS you'll be notified of special **one day only fan pricing** on new releases.

Sign up today to get free stories.

CLICK HERE

or visit: https://marthacarr.com/read-free-stories/

This weekend seven authors will join me in the 2nd Austin Author Summit to create a hive mind where we can share ideas, problems we just can't solve, and our plans for the immediate future. I got the idea for a small group from a vision of how we all generally stare at our own problems – from very close up. I call it standing too close to the wallpaper to see the pattern right in front of your face.

But if I mention that tangled knot to someone else who has no stake in my game, they often light up with an obvious solution.

Plus, I didn't want to have to fly somewhere so hosting the summit in my home seemed brilliant... Bonus points – I get to show off the dream house.

Anyway, back to the real benefits of this plan and how you can adopt it in your life as well. It's an opportunity to practice vulnerability, which requires telling the absolute truth. Not the partial truth that doesn't quite expose how afraid we might be, or that one decision that's kinda haunting you right now, or even that bold move you made that you think will work out but you really don't need anyone poking at it. Those bugs under our rock that if only we could talk about them, they wouldn't seem so hairy.

Instead of staring at the edges of what looks like it could become a problem, I'm gathering in a few select people to talk about solutions. What can't be solved or altered or changed in any way, I can let go. That's the parts I'm powerless over – but not a victim because I'm taking care of business where I can.

I can use weekends like this because not only am I an author – I'm an entrepreneur and the business side only grows more complex with new layers all the time. And this is a role I didn't see coming. Every day is new territory, which requires a lot of letting go and planning and working with others and at the end of the day, trusting that all is well. Some days that last part is harder to do than on other days. It's always easier with a small group of people walking that same road.

And there's a Part 2, of course… Everyone shares some corner of the world where they've figured out things, helping everyone else. I'm going to talk about creating an infrastructure for my business – it's been a year and I've learned a few things. I'm looking forward to learning a few new things too.

Then there's the future plans where we can encourage each other to dream and throw our support and ideas behind the magic castle each of us is building every day. Even better, the small group of hard-working authors will get the chance to bond and know each other better and build friendships that can go the distance. More adventures to follow.

Thank you for reading our stories. Without readers, being a creative author is a very lonely existence. You help make everything we do seem bathed in sunshine!

A couple of years ago, Craig Martelle wanted to 'do an author convention right.' We might have had maybe 8,000 people in the 20Booksto50k® author group I started at the time.

I honestly don't remember, but it shouldn't have been much more than that – we have 34,000 now.

The first convention was 400 attendees, and it was a fantabulous time! I wasn't living in Vegas when the heavy lifting of locating a venue needed to be accomplished. So, I needed someone who loved Vegas.

I knew *JUST* the person!

Walking into my bedroom, I sought out Judith Anderle (whose Match.com name included the letters 'lovesVegas' when I met her – I should know, I met her on Match.)

I asked if she would be willing to go to Vegas to help the

group, she questioned 'how soon' and I probably said something 'mumble mumble can you go soon?'

My cell phone rang. "One minute baby," I called out, looking around for my cell phone. Finding it, I picked it up. "Hello?"

Judith was on the phone. "It's me baby, I'm here in Vegas. What do you need me to do?"

I stared at the phone… I stared at where she had been standing just moments before and wondered *how in the world did she get there so fast?*

Sometimes, the person who can help lives in the same house as you. Often, they don't.

But, we are still using the hotel Judith found (Sam's Town) for our third year when about 1,200 attendees along with major companies in the Indie Publishing Industry will gather together, learn from each other and help figure out how to provide YOU readers with more of what you love best.

Reading!

So, whether you build something in your home, or a conference (which was Craig Martelle's hard work, not mine) always seek to bring people into your life that can help you get up to the top of your mountain.

Life is amazing. You just have to be willing to open yourself up to what it can bring you and #probably do a few things that are uncomfortable.

Until next time ;-)

Michael

OTHER BOOKS BY JUDITH BERENS

OTHER BOOKS BY MARTHA CARR

JOIN THE ORICERAN UNIVERSE FAN GROUP ON FACEBOOK!

BOOKS BY MICHAEL ANDERLE

For a complete list of books by Michael Anderle, please visit

www.lmbpn.com/ma-books/

All LMBPN Audiobooks are Available at Audible.com and iTunes. For a complete list of audiobooks visit:

www.lmbpn.com/audible

www.ingramcontent.com/pod-product-compliance
Lightning Source LLC
Chambersburg PA
CBHW050245110726
47898CB00007B/2282